An

B

CW01572564

A No... ...y ....

By S.E. Foulk

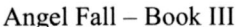

This is a work of fiction. All of the characters, organizations, and events portrayed in this novel are either products of the author's imagination or are used fictitiously.

Cover Art: *Lucifer, King of Hell*, by Paul Gustave Doré, circa 1861-1868

ISBN-13: 978-1468063592
ISBN-10: 1468063596

First Edition: December 2011

Dedicated

to my Mom,

Marjory Steiner,

*who surprisingly liked this story even though she just read
it to be a good mother,
and now battles cancer with the help of her faithful dog,
Andy.*

Happily, she is winning the fight!

Go Mom!

Acknowledgement

This book, as well as Book I and Book II, was edited by my wife, C. Mamo Kim, PhD., and would not have been possible to get out otherwise.

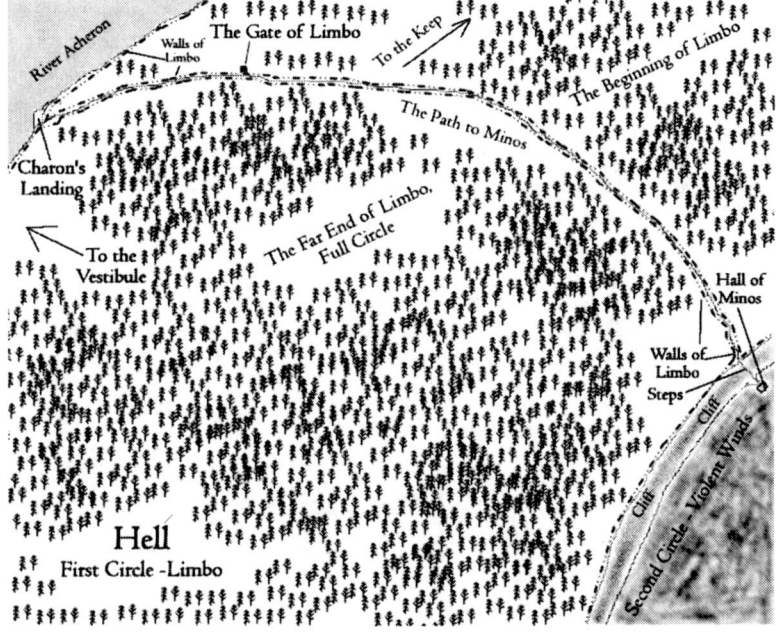

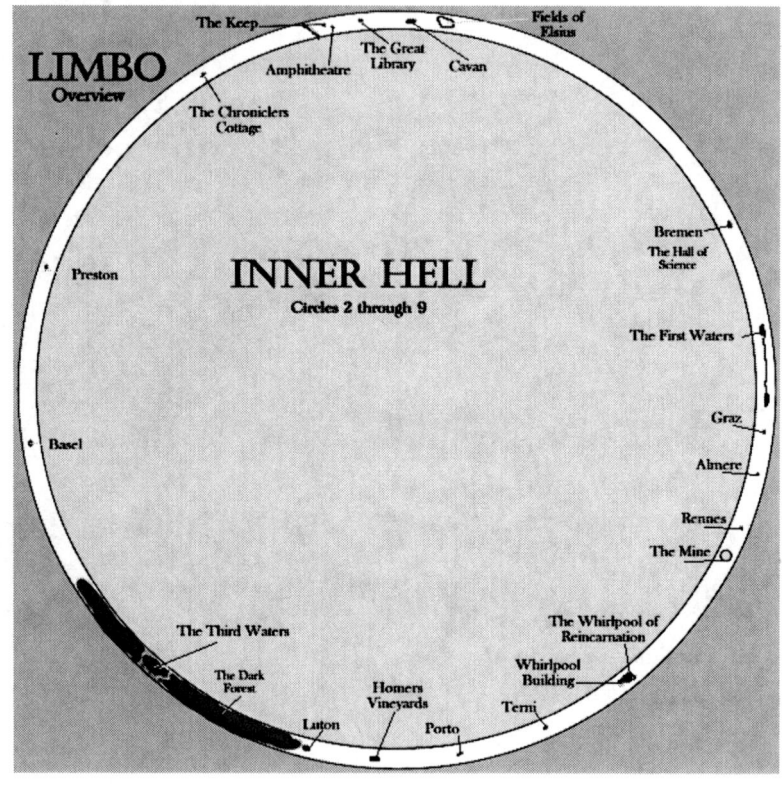

Prelude

A Fateful End

I stood there, watching in surprise. I was in a very long line, the line that leads into the Hall of Minos, where I was to be judged and sentenced for all of eternity. I had gathered this much since entering the place, having been a once ardent fan of Dante's Inferno, though a few things were off, like the high walls on both sides of this path. I did not have time to think out or consider the differences, because even if I was not in the Inferno, I was surely in Hell somewhere. And that weighed upon me beyond comprehension. The sounds of thrashing, violent winds grew ominously louder, and I felt the foul air brush against my face. Far ahead, where the line neared the Hall entrance, a huge centaur had appeared out of the darkness, trotting toward the line, where a commotion was scattering the once orderly, almost sluggish line. I could not see at first; the people ahead stood in the way and the drop was too shallow to catch a glance. But as the crowd began to part, I finally spotted a lone man at the center of the crowd. He was shrieking in anguish and terror as a pair of toddler-sized, discolored creatures, maybe three feet high, tore away at his flesh with claws and rows of razor-sharp teeth.

The centaur was huge. If he were all man or all horse, he would be considered large, from head to haunches. His musculature was that of a body builder, only naturally built, not of the steroid variety. The centaur was bleeding from its shoulder as he walked straight at the melee. In hand, the centaur had a large thick bow, and was stringing an arrow while keeping his eyes locked on the hideous blood frenzy. Just as I thought he was going to shoot off the arrow, there was a loud noise that came from the building; like a roar, only with a human-like voice. The air trembled. I was reminded of my Uncle Rich, who had a booming timber when he spoke. Uncle Rich had a unique sound I'd heard rarely in my life. This new voice, however, was seriously frightening. The whole line, previously panicked and reacting to the sight of the blood fest, got very quiet, very fast, and only the sound of the blowing winds from behind the hall could be heard. Even the centaur, intimidating as he was, stopped and lowered his bow. Then, out of the building and down the steps came a human who was as muscular as the centaur. He looked to be in his fifties, darkly tanned, with huge arms and torso muscles, extremely well defined, and a powerful, square jaw and weathered face. Like the centaur, he was shirtless. From where I stood, I guessed he was about six foot eight, but I recalled meeting a professional basketball player once who was the same height, only the basketball player was nowhere near as wide and muscular as this guy. I watched just as quietly as everyone else, the man approach the centaur, wondering if I should expect a fight. If they did fight, I wanted to be out of striking distance. I was still recovering from getting my brains bashed in by Charon.

Before he became aware of the centaur's presence, the big man had shouted at the small beasts, stopping short in his surprise. The strong winds from behind the Hall were incredibly loud, increasing and decreasing sporadically. I could hear the two exchanging words that were too muffled to discern. They spoke briefly before the centaur finally turned back toward the man who was being attacked by the rabid beasts. The centaur raised the large bow but I did not see him aim or fire. I saw one of the beasts that had climbed onto the screaming mans shoulder, suddenly grasping at its own throat, trying to remove an arrow which had magically materialized there. The centaur had moved that fast, and that precisely. A few inches less and the beast's victim would have had the shaft through his head. The pierced beast stood, frantically trying to pull the arrow out when in seconds, still holding its shape, it transformed into a black cloud; another second later and it was gone, the blowing winds dispersing the smoke rapidly.

At that point, the powerful man said something to the centaur, then waved his arms as if performing a magic show trick with great flamboyance. He spoke words, again, which I could not make out. A strange light went off in my head and the second creature became a smoke cloud, dispersing in the wind. The centaur seemed to relax a little, and the crowd, recognizing the disturbance was over, was eager to move away from the still screaming man and return to their previous, orderly line. Everyone continued to gawk at the commanding pair until they disappeared into the Hall.

No longer bored with this line, I stood in anxious anticipation, as if a giant wave was coming at me. I remembered I was fast approaching my sentence.

Eternity was near.

Chapter 46

Fatherhood

Chiron's visit with Minos lasted a long time, and only after

deciding he could trust the thunder-voiced human would Chiron

divulge his reasons for traveling to Limbo. Originally, he was afraid

Minos would be a cantankerous old fool, untrustworthy and too

pompous to deal with; instead, the two hit it off as if they had been old

friends. Each shared his stories from life, and each had details to tell the

other about their experiences of Hell. They sat in the Great Hall, in a

section that was behind the pillars, and out of sight of the line of new

arrivals. A doorway off to the right of the pillars contained a large

throne, and Minos sat while Chiron stood on all fours. There were

chairs for company, but none that would accommodate a Halfling form.

The large room was empty except for three chairs, a large mirror,

ornately decorated with gold carvings of winged humans and strange,

beautiful beasts, and the two new friends. Chiron was impressed by the

workmanship of the carvings, and mysteriously compelled to look into the mirror. When Chiron moved in front of the mirror, Minos gave him an ominous warning.

"Do not get too close to it, Lord Chiron. I do not know what effect it would have upon you, being a centaur, but I prefer not to lose your company prematurely. It is enchanted and would send you away from here should you look into it too long." With decided urgency, Minos commanded. "Please come away from it for your own good."

Chiron did as he was told, not wishing to be transported when he was so near to Limbo. As the pair conversed, newcomer humans came into the room and walked to the mirror. Chiron watched as the people would stare into the glass, mesmerized for a few minutes, and then vanish. After, Minos would roar "NEXT" and another human would enter the room. Minos turned back toward the conversation as if nothing had happened.

"And how is it you know Aristotle is being held in the cave near you?" asked Minos.

"My commander, Nessus, informed me. I ordered him to watch the area, as he is the least distractible of all my sentries." Chiron seemed to be bothered as he mentioned Nessus, and his discomfort was visible to Minos.

"My friend, who is Nessus, your fellow centaur? Why do you seem pained at the mention of his name?"

"It is nothing, Minos," said Chiron, but his body language, at least from his human torso up, spoke otherwise.

"You distrust Nessus. It is obvious, my friend." Chiron knew he was cornered in the conversation, and decided to open to the ancient king.

"I confess that I do not trust Nessus, nor does my second, Pholus."

"What has he perpetrated to earn your distrust, Master Centaur?"

"I am loath to speak of it, Minos. I haven't any real proof, only hearsay and my own intuition. I would not speak of it harshly until I do so."

"Surely you can speak of what evidence you have, be it hearsay or feeling, without slandering your fellow." Chiron, thinking about Minos' words for a moment, decided it would not be unfair to express his own reasoning and doubts.

"Very well Minos. It will do me good to be rid of it after so many centuries. There are two issues I can speak about, and, as I have said, they are based on hearsay and circumstance. First, I believe that Nessus desires my position as head of the centaur race. I hear stirrings from time to time, and once I was even challenged to physical combat by an oaf who is so lacking in basic intelligence I know he could not possibly have imagined a challenge of his own accord. Furthermore, investigations were initiated whenever these stirrings rose in intensity, and each time Nessus' name came up somewhere in the controversy. Yet, when I question him, he always has a solid alibi, and proclaims his innocence and lack of knowledge."

"You believe he is after your position?" asked Minos.

"Yes I do. And I would gladly hand it to him if I could leave this place."

"Why don't you let him have it now?" asked Minos.

"I knew of Nessus in life, Minos. He may have betrayed his fellow centaurs to the humans who slaughtered our kind in order to save his own skin; which leads me to the next item for which I do not trust him. I believe Nessus reports to the Fallen." Minos looked surprised.

"What evidence have you?" asked Minos.

"The harpies. In my circle, the harpies hate only one thing more than they hate my kind, and that is the Fallen. When Fallen appear, harpies disappear. It's as if the harpies can sense or smell the Fallen; they always disappear just before the Fallen arrive."

14

"How does this tie into Nessus?"

"Nessus stays on the far side of Phlegethon, usually observing the forbidden area cave. On one occasion, he was required to cross over to meet with Pholus, my second in command, and I. When we travel to the wooded side of Phlegethon, the harpies are always present, watching from a distance. When Nessus was coming to meet us, I had noticed the harpies, in fact a few of them, sitting in the tree tops; they ate silently, eyes on the herds warily, but disengaged. As Nessus was approaching, however, I detected many sharp movements out of the corner of my eye, and the harpies quickly vanished altogether. It took me awhile to put it together, but it makes sense to me that Nessus, in his duty as watcher of the forbidden area, has consorted with Fallen. I believe this is the case."

"It is a terrible thing to – NEXT! – not trust your subordinates. My palace was full of treachery between the servants, and between the nobles, who often attempted to manipulate me to distrust their peers. I was foolishly coerced many times, even having one of my servants beaten for a crime he did not commit. I almost executed a noble for the same reason."

15

A large man entered the room and walked to the mirror. Chiron could see the partial reflection of the man, and as the man began having a tantrum, cursing and trying to pound the glass, Chiron noticed the mirror's reflection steadily blackening and flowing like liquid; Chiron could smell the unmistakable stench of the Styx coming from the mirror. The upset man vanished, and the mirror returned to normal. Minos did not seem fazed by the incident, and continued his story.

"NEXT! When I learned of this treachery, I spoke no more to my servants and instead hired a master who would manage them directly. The perpetrator - JUST WALK OVER TO THE MIRROR - who fooled me into beating the servant was released. He jumped to his death shortly thereafter. It was a shame. They have such small lives."

The next man, small and skinny, moved so slowly that Chiron thought Minos would go over and throw him at the mirror.

"MOVE!"

The king kept talking, and the man finally reached the front of the mirror in tears as he anticipated his torment. Chiron saw the mirror change quickly, only this time it looked like the place he had seen in his vision, the icy area. The skinny man cried out and bowed his head, and then was gone instantly. The mirror returned to its normal state.

16

"NEXT!" roared Minos. The individual humans continued to enter the room and evoke the powers of the mirror. In some cases, Chiron saw the moaning woods that bordered his river. Other times the red river itself appeared, or the fiery plain beyond the wood. Another time it was the tomb area, and many times there were areas he did not know. In each case, scents and odors came from the mirror which Chiron knew emanated from the site shown to the human. All the smells were different, and usually foul. In just one case there was a scene and a scent that was so pleasant that Chiron could not help but stop listening to the king. He had detected a trace of the scent on Aristotle once, but it was so polluted with the odors of outer Hell that the Master Centaur could not tell if it was real or he had imagined it. Minos smiled as he saw Chiron's distraction at the pleasantness.

"Limbo," said the smiling king. "It is very rare, but still happens every couple of hundred years. Smells wonderful."

Chiron sniffed loudly, taking in the smell of fresh forest and field as the man disappeared. The scent disappeared immediately, disappointing Chiron momentarily. The two masters continued their seemingly endless chat, where, after much talk that

17

wandered far from the original subject, Chiron became comfortable enough to discuss the matter of Asterion with Minos. He had been uncertain earlier on, but the king seemed genuinely happy to see Chiron, and opened himself up to the point where the Master Centaur knew Minos could be trusted.

"Minos, I would speak to you of your son." The king looked away, suddenly distracted by the mirror and its next victim for the first time since the centaur's arrival. Chiron could feel Minos cringing, though he continued. "I realize this is an uncomfortable topic, but I am compelled to speak of it, as I have promised. Minos, I have met your son, in the Sixth Circle." Minos grew pale and suddenly acted as an adolescent, shying away from an accusing parent. Chiron, originally fearful of how the great judge of Hell would respond, smiled to himself.

"He is not my son, Chiron. I have been made aware of the presence of Asterion in the tombs – I caught a fugitive, who told me many things about the circles and creatures below before I summoned the Fallen." Minos was scowling at the mention of the Fallen. "Asterion was the son of my wife and the accursed bull-''

"He is *your* son, Minos. I can assure you of that." Chiron was direct, and looked straight at Minos, who was now reddening.

"And how is it that you know this, Chiron?" Minos' anger stirred, but he kept his voice in check. "I have no bovine lineage to speak of and my advisor informed me that my wife had been with the bull-"

"Could your advisor have been lying to you? I saw Asterion, and I know he is your son. We centaurs have senses that are far more acute than that of humans, Minos. I can detect familiar scents, my eyes are sharper, and I can see his parentage clearly, especially after seeing you. I know he is your son. Have you ever consulted with anyone outside of your advisor?"

"My advisor was highly trustworthy, Chiron. He saved my life once, when we were children. His parents were of noble lineage, and he had the deepest regard for my wife. I would dare say he loved her himself! Were I not king he would have certainly married her first. Reporting that she was with the bull was so very difficult for him, I could tell just by his stammering, his pleading for me to forgive him for having to report such an aberration of behavior." Minos looked at the floor briefly and then straight ahead with determination.

"Still, I took care of the beast-child, and I give my regard to you; I only say 'beast' because that was his nature, not because he is a Halfling. The child ripped out my advisor's heart one day, and devoured it in front of his dying eyes. The advisor was charged with taming Asterion for public appearances, for his own good. Asterion would have no kindness, only blood. I had very little choice; either slay him or condemn him to spend his life in the labyrinth. I chose the latter."

"And you trusted the advisor with the boy?"

"He was the bastard son of the bull and more feral than other Halflings. My advisor assured me he had no intelligence beyond the ability to hate and to kill humans! The child murdered my friend and was found over the body, eating the man's heart! And this even after my advisor had given him much care and personal attention."

Chiron shook his head knowingly. He was hearing all the same rhetoric used to justify the extermination of his kind, and the anger and disgust he felt was being rekindled. Minos was highly irritated by Chiron's head shaking, and burst out in anger before he could control himself.

"Do not shake your head at me! The child was a killer!" Minos took some deep breaths. "Why do you not you believe me, Chiron? I realize you were persecuted in life for your parentage, but you were not of wild, violent disposition. Look how well you did for yourself – you

are highly respected by kings and gods alike. Asterion was not near
your temperament or intellect."

Minos trailed off. He was not happy to have lost his temper, and
over the thousands of years he had much time to consider a number of
issues in his lifetime, including the matter of Asterion. Questions had
surfaced again and again, but the king kept telling himself he *had* taken
the appropriate measures, he *had* done the right thing, he *had* done the
best for all concerned. But now it was evident to Minos that the subject
of Asterion was not fully resolved within him. The mere mention of the
bull Halfling had unsettled him beyond the many reasonable facts he
had been ruminating over for millennia.

"Minos," Chiron paused, looking into the pained eyes of the
former king. "You do not know the persecution I went through in life. I
was nearly slain by humans on many occasions, and were it not for my
special parentage, I would have perished long before making a name in
the world of the living. I will speak to you plainly, and I would have
you listen. I respect you, and your position, but I must impose what I
understand to be the truth. Will you listen, and listen only, until I
finish?"

"Of course." replied Minos quietly, held in the eyes of the centaur.

21

"I have another sense, a sense of character assessment, which I have had since birth. This sense of assessment has helped me dealing with many humans and centaurs alike, and I trust and regard it highly. Many times while growing up, I was warned, and I disregarded this sense for what was before my eyes. I gave more weight to what I saw rather than what I sensed. This led to betrayal by those whom I trusted, and I so wanted to trust."

"When I finally began to trust in my ability, the world changed for the better, minus the attempts on my life by those who were threatened by my ability." Chiron paused again, and looked at Minos so that the king could not pull his gaze away, pinning him with his eyes. "Asterion is your son. Not of the bull, or of anything other than some malevolent magic aimed at you and your wife. I sense the magical and I know Asterion is a human child, cursed at birth or just before, and transformed into the Minotaur. The spell was singular and irreversible in effect. You must have had a great enemy. This is powerful magic that can hold from birth and throughout even death."

Minos was squirming with the discomfort and shock of this revelation.

Memories of situations where he had questioned his advisor-friend, and was given answers that seemed to conflict flooded his mind. Minos never bothered to inquire more deeply because Asterion and his deformity had always pained the great King. He had been awaiting the birth of a beautiful son, and the monstrosity that birthed from his wife's loins horrified and wounded him greatly. He did not know of the incident of the bull and his wife until his friend, the advisor, reluctantly spoke of it. Until then he had been terribly saddened, but coped as best as he could because his wife kept the child close to her, caring for it tenderly. Eventually, the advisor persuaded Minos to conceal the half bull from the eyes of the nobles. Minos' wife wept for weeks, and after a month threw herself from the palace walls. The king recalled with no small amount of guilt how his hatred for the child grew uncontrollably after that and how he completely relinquished the child to the care of his advisor, who convinced the king to banish the child from memory.

Now the legendary Chiron was confirming what Minos had been seeking to bury and deny. It felt true. The king was stunned. What else did the Master Centaur know, he wondered.

"Minos - Asterion was a wild, unmerciful killer who fed on his victims." Minos didn't move a muscle. "Asterion was *raised* to become a killer… made into a killer…trained and brutalized by someone, who I now know was your advisor. Have you ever seen a dog raised to attack and kill? Dogs are domesticated, and will do what they are trained to do. If the dog is beaten, it becomes mean, and lives only to survive. Asterion was treated similarly, and lived to survive."

"I spoke to your son. He followed me into the Sixth Circle, and I do not know if he intended to attack or only wanted to study me. He could not believe my kindness toward him. He shared his stories, the only stories he knew, stories of his upbringing, beatings and captivity. Your advisor treated him so badly that he wanted only to die. He wished to die. But in his rage, your son destroyed the man who destroyed his soul. For this, he was sentenced to the labyrinth by you, and was given a reputation not of his own making." Chiron stopped. Minos had just enough energy to look away.

"Interestingly, we were on the topic of distrust of those whose loyalty should be unwavering. Tell me, Minos, what was the name of your friend, the advisor?" asked Chiron. The king spoke softly, as if he did not want to be heard, but his reply did not escape the sharp hearing of the centaur.

"His name was Garum."

24

Chapter 47

The Missing Ferryman

The centaur could feel it; the anguish that had been trapped inside

of the king - now judge of the dead - welled deep and, surging like

waves, overflowed like a slow, powerful tsunami. The enormity of his

anguish caused Minos body to convulse spasmodically. Chiron stepped

away, trotting outside the room to allow the proud king his privacy.

Hell was the land of tears and anguish, guilt and regret. It was a human

land.

Chiron stopped short. The line to the great hall was gone. Formerly

filled with the newly arrived humans waiting for judgment, it was now

vast and empty. The quiet was not natural for this place; most would be

weeping as they got closer to their eternal sentence. The hall had an

eerie low tone; only the wind could be heard as it whistled across and

around the back of the structure. Chiron wanted to tell Minos, but the

king needed this time alone. Chiron stood quietly, inspecting his

wounds that had been inflicted by the imps behind the Hall earlier, to

see how they had healed since beginning his conversation with Minos;

it had been quite a while. They had closed up and only the dried blood that had flowed from the lacerations indicated that any damage had occurred. He wiped the crusted blood away mindlessly when, in an instant, the silence was broken by Minos, roaring through his sobs.

"NEXT!" Silence, then after a short pause. "NEXT!" Chiron watched as Minos stormed out from the mirror room, swollen red eyes glaring at the empty hall. "What is this?! No!" Minos looked around, behind pillars as if the people would be hiding from him. "Where are the people Chiron? Chiron?" The king stared at Chiron as if he were hiding the people himself.

"The Hall was empty when I arrived, Minos. I do not know why. The line must have finished as we spoke." The two walked to the steps and out onto the path leading up to the First Circle. Minos was looking around frantically, in complete disbelief.

"This has never happened. I am not sure what to do!" Minos looked into the air, walked around behind the hall, and returned back to the front steps, frantically searching for what could have happened to the line. "I am afraid I will have to summon the Fallen, Chiron. You must leave this area."

"Minos, can you withhold your summons, for just a short time? I would investigate further were I you. Perhaps talk to Charon, despite his temperament. He may know something we do not."

"Yes - yes" said the frantic judge. A very good idea. I would walk with you up to the gate. They would not let you in alone I fear, but I have friends there, and they will not deny me entry. If they do not allow you entrance, I will intercede. Let us walk. I am growing more concerned"

The two quickly walked up the steps to the walls that formed the corridor of the path. Soon they came to the gates, as Minos continued speaking.

"I would help you further were the burden of my fear lifted; I am not finished with our conversation, but you have given me some release, and I would speak with you longer. Would you walk with me to Acheron, and stand with me while I question Charon? Your presence may help to stifle his gargantuan rudeness and temper. You have nothing to fear as long as you do not touch his boat or his person. I will properly introduce you as a co-worker of Hell, and he will not threaten you. He suspects everyone as being a fugitive, though I have heard he

will transport anyone for an object of worth. I don't know why since he
has no use for valuable objects. Perhaps old habits die hard."

Chiron considered the request of Minos and recognized he might
not be able to venture outside of the Seventh Circle ever again, he
wanted to see more. Thousands of years of boredom made his decision
certain.

"I will assist you, Minos. Let us go see the ferryman." Minos
smiled briefly, and the two set off up the path to the river Acheron,
reaching it after a long walk. When they arrived, Minos shock
worsened. Sitting on the shore was the skiff of Charon, but there was
no sign of the volatile ferryman to be found.

"Perhaps Charon has taken a break, or is off on his own journey?"
offered Chiron.

"Charon has no adventuring spirit within him, Chiron. He is a
creature of cold habit, never changing, intolerant to any new difficulty
or challenge. It is what makes him a miserable old fool, and he clings to
it steadfastly." Minos paused in thought. "Would you like to come to
the far shore, Chiron? We can take the skiff and-"

"I would not be comfortable in this 'skiff' Minos. I was able to
cross the Styx by way of Phlegyas, but only because I had no other

28

choice. I believe I should return to my task before I am discovered by those who will soon be missing Charon. I must leave now for the gate."

"Wait my friend. I will help get you passage into Limbo as I said." Minos looked furtively around, "I would warn you also, you must not tell the Elders of the problem with Charon - I suspect the leaders of Limbo have too much loyalty to Fallen, and I would still prefer to solve this riddle myself, before we are overrun with their worker demons and imps." Minos looked straight at Chiron, seriousness in his eyes. "Chiron, that spell I cast on the imp earlier - it is forbidden. If the Fallen were ever to know that I had used their magic, I would be sentenced to one of the punishments in the depths far below, maybe in your forbidden area, or deeper. Do not use the spell in front of anyone you do not fully trust; I believe in your sense of character and I would trust you to rely heavily upon it. That incantation is the only other way to destroy the demons and vermin imps, though for demons it may not be as subtle as you have witnessed. I do not casually cast this spell. I have had no company for some time, and thought to impress you with my knowledge. I am a fool for showing off. The spell will work only on the demons and imps and not humans or any other creatures of Hell.

Have a care, Chiron. It may come in handy in your travels. Now, let us go."

Back they walked along the path until they reached the giant iron gate of Limbo again. Minos motioned Chiron to stand back while he knocked loudly on the great metal doorway. In a few moments, a plate slid away and the eyes of a guard looked out at the king. The eyes stared and grew large as he saw the formidable size of the powerful judge of Hell, then appeared to consider before finally speaking.

"Greetings sir. You are King Minos?"

"Yes, I am he, my good fellow, though king no more…for quite some time. I do appreciate your respectfulness, however." Minos smiled. He was happy to socialize, especially if it would further Chiron's chances of entry into Limbo. A little charm could spare a thousand soldiers, his mother would say.

"Your highness," said a deep voice from the gate, trying to emit respect in his tones. "Pardon me for not opening the gateway. We have recent orders to inspect our guests first. We are honored."

"Greetings to you my friend." returned Minos. "Please open the gate. I would ask a favor of you, friend guard."

"Yes sir!" replied the guards voice; he had stepped away in order to open the gate. The plate slid back into place, just as the gateway opened wide. The guard looked at Minos, and was smiling when he saw the large form of Chiron standing at the side. "Your highness! What is -" exclaimed the stunned guard. Minos noted the shock of the guard, and seized the moment.

"My friend, this is Master Chiron, leader of the centaurs of the Seventh Circle and a proper worker of Hell, as am I. He is also a friend to Limbo's citizenry. I came to ask you to allow him entry – he is on a brief task, and will only remain within your walls temporarily." The guard stood staring at the Master Centaur, mouth agape. "Will you permit my friend, Lord Chiron, entry into Limbo, friend guard? I will assume full responsibility."

"Yes, your highness, sir. It would be our great pleasure to entertain any guest you send us and we are much honored to have one so well known and revered! I do not need to inform the Elders, they will find out soon enough, and it will be to their delight, I assure you." The guard turned to Chiron, bowing his head in reverence. "Please, enter Master Chiron. I will accompany you personally, and take you wherever you wish to go. Which Elder is it that you seek?"

"I seek Socius, ward of Aristotle." said Chiron. The guard smiled.

"Socius? We all know of Socius - he is friend to many. Please, Master Chiron, enter and enjoy our air and environment." The guard turned to Minos. "Your highness, you are also welcome. It would be a double honor for us." Minos smiled at this.

"I will visit my friend, though not this time. I have my own tasks which I cannot ignore. Thank you for allowing my friend. May the Gods honor you." Minos waved to Chiron, and then started back toward his hall.

"Goodbye my friend." said Chiron as he watched the king leave. Minos was going back to his hall to investigate before summoning the Fallen. Chiron would have liked to see the reaction of the Fallen himself, but since he was out of his assigned territory, it would be a very bad idea. They might transform him into some monstrous mad centaur-demon, as they had turned Plutus into the wolf-demon.

Chiron watched his new friend disappear down the path. The guard waited, smiling, and the inner gate was opened by his fellows, revealing a grassy, green, earthy smelling Limbo. The other guards, like the gatekeeper, stared in awe at the massive centaur. None had ever seen a centaur, and now they were being visited by the master of all centaurs, the legendary Chiron. They stood agape as he walked regally past them and into Limbo. People who had been engaged in conversations with each other stopped and stared in disbelief of their own senses. Chiron saw all their shocked faces, but was involved with the scents he had barely experienced before when he stood in the mirror room of Minos' hall. He was enraptured as his nostrils snorted and breathed the earthy scented clean air of Limbo.

"Master Chiron, I see you are enjoying our fresh air. Please follow me." said the guard. "As I promised, I will take you to Socius personally."

"Thank you friend. I will enjoy your environment as we walk. Is it a distant journey to where Socius dwells?" asked Chiron. He would prefer it to be very long, as he took in the sights and smells.

"Master Chiron, Socius normally dwells nearby the gate, particularly when he awaits Aristotle, but he has recently taken a journey to the far side of Limbo, and we will have to walk for a long distance. We can stop at the First Waters along the way; they will refresh you unlike any other." The guard could not believe his luck. Here, walking along with him was the legendary Chiron. In the childhood of his lifetime, the warrior had been told many stories about the ancient heroes and characters. He was in a haze, a dream state, and he thought he would be better off not to awaken from it. If he would escort the great Chiron, let the way be long.

Chiron smiled. He had not been certain that he would be welcomed, and now he was being escorted into Limbo as an honored guest. The trees were real - different, but real, unlike the bleeding, moaning trees the harpies lived in and fed from. As he walked near a large tree, he sniffed the air to lavish the scent of it. A centaur's sense of smell, far keener than a human, allowed Chiron to smell not only the leaves, but the trunk, the bark and the oils produced within. It was remarkable and healing just to be inside of Limbo, an aromatherapy he had taken for granted in life. Chiron wanted to take his time and dwell in this intoxicating atmosphere, but he would do what he came to do, above all. Surely his exit would be a sad occasion.

"Guard," asked Chiron. "I would prefer to not be involved with the Elders at this time. Is it possible we can circumvent the structure known as the Keep? I am in urgent need of speaking to Socius, and then I must exit Limbo in haste. I hope your leaders will understand. Should I be able to make a diplomatic journey and return, I will follow the proper protocol. For now, I must get to Socius as soon as possible. I would be

discrete, though I see that is no longer an option." Chiron looked
around as the few people in the area had all stopped their conversations,
agape as he stood with the guard. Even the guards behind him had not
closed the entry way into Limbo because they did not wish to lose sight
of the Master Centaur.

"Lord Chiron, it is my honor to escort you as you wish. We can
move in less popular pathways to reach Socius, and I will ask other
guards to assist so we can pass through without interruption." said the
guard. Chiron smiled and nodded his head.

"That would be my preference, friend guard." replied Chiron.

"It is my honor, sir. And please call me Nigel." said the guard.

"Thanks to you, Nigel. Lead on." Chiron and the guard turned to
the right, and walked a narrow path toward the wall that bordered the
Second Circle, and he could hear the winds faintly with his keen
centaur hearing. Soon, they were alone on the path, and concealed by
more medium sized trees. Chiron saw only trees and wall, and he
delighted in the environment as they journeyed. He thought of his
human friend, and asked questions of himself. Why would Aristotle
ever leave Limbo for outer Hell? What had he found that threatened the
Fallen? What could possibly have happened to Charon? He did not

distract himself with the thoughts for long, however. Chiron wanted most of all to spend his time enjoying the refreshing air and scenery, savoring his temporary bliss.

He felt renewed.

Chapter 48

Panos and the Centaurs

Panos could barely see. The strange demon bird creatures had swooped down on him just as he spotted the red river. They had pinned him down, shredding his chest and abdomen and disemboweling him viciously strokes with their razor-like talons. Panos had immediately feared he would encounter trouble from the herd of centaurs he'd seen standing in the distance when he emerged from the moaning trees. He had not seen the bird demons coming.

Now, Panos lay on the ground, surrounded by the Halflings. He could hear them talking, but could not yet see; he was blinded in one eye, which had been ripped out by the bird beasts in their frenzy, and blood flowing from the other wounds on his face interfered with the sight of his remaining eye. Panos wondered if his eye was gone for good or if it was still hanging there. He heard the deliberate trotting of one of the centaurs coming toward him, and then a commotion of hooves in slight movement, as if giving way to the newcomer.

"Greetings Commander Pholus!" said Equus, the leader of the herd that had inadvertently rescued the human from the harpies.

"Equus," replied Pholus, approaching the bloody mess that was Panos. Pholus looked down at the mutilated human, sniffing the air around Panos, analyzing it to discern his origins.

"Then it is true, Equus. I could hardly believe it when Titan informed me. We will have to wait for the regeneration to complete before we get any information from this fugitive. Do not blow the horn; we need to find out how and why this human is here." Pholus studied his wounds. "They have really mangled his face, nasty, crude beasts. They are still angry at our battle victory, and apparently have taken it out on the human."

Pholus threw this out for the benefit of the herd as a reminder of their recent battle. He knew they would take it well, and predictably, the centaurs cheered in unison, taking in the compliment to their battle prowess. "At least the harpies were smart enough to flee when your command arrived. They may have some intelligence to them after all."

"Master Pholus, should we not report this to Master Chiron?" asked another centaur. The herds were not aware that Chiron had journeyed to the First Circle to get answers about his human friend,

Aristotle. They did not know Aristotle was being held and tortured in the forbidden area.

"Yes, Equus. I will inform Master Chiron," replied Pholus. "Have Titan report to me at the forbidden area cave when this human can speak, but do not question him until I arrive. I would hear his answers firsthand." Pholus looked at Panos, who had been listening intently. The weakened human had lost the ability to move his arms. The muscles in his arms had also been shredded away, and so he could not even wipe the blood pooling uncomfortably on his face. "Equus," said Pholus, "Do not allow any harm to come to him. We need answers before we contact the Fallen. There are strange occurrences happening in Hell and we must be cautious for now." Then Pholus turned and headed back toward the shallows. The herd resumed speaking among themselves.

Panos sighed in relief as he heard the centaur trot away. He would have some peace while he regenerated. He was grateful for that. Exhausted and in pain as he was, he marveled at being in the presence of what he had always believed were but mythical creatures.

Centaurs had held Panos' imagination even while he lived as a boy in the old countryside. Yet once he regenerated and answered their questions, Hell would come for him once more in the form of the Fallen. Panos tried to relax into his regeneration aware of one important thing.

He must escape.

Chapter 49

Identification

Mortuus could hardly believe what the dwarfish Clavius had just told him. He swooned, unable to digest the news. Clavius was shouting something to the laboratory assistants, but it was indecipherable to Mortuus, who could not grasp spoken language in this moment. Words were sounding like grunts and groans in the ether. Socius and Barak had already jumped up on either side of Mortuus, each grabbing an arm and supporting his large, limp frame as best as they could. Darius moved behind Mortuus, propping him up with both hands. Clavius two assistants exited, running into a small hallway.

"Mortuus! Mortuus!" everyone was shouting, trying to bring their friend's balance back. Mortuus went limp for a second. Barak strained to hold him up; Mortuus was quite heavy. Just as quickly as his legs had buckled under him, Mortuus willed himself to consciousness as if fighting off sleep.

"Clavius, you are certain then?" asked a groaning Barak. "I have heard this theory, but I have not seen any evidence to conclude that Mortuus..." He was loath to say what Barak had just told them.

Mortuus was one of the Fallen.

Barak had been astounded when Mortuus destroyed the demon, but automatically attributed it to two intersecting trajectories; one, the fact that the demon was in an unusually weakened state because it was under the spell of transformation, and two, that Mortuus was unusually large in frame. It was a great victory, but certainly only an extreme human accomplishment, so he thought.

"There is plenty of evidence. You related the first sign of it to me, and the runner, whom you recently saw pass the whirlpool house has confirmed it. The theory is sound. The Chronicler had sent the runner to find Mortuus before the demons could," Clavius spoke firmly. Barak tried to rationalize all the various bits of information pertaining to Mortuus that he could think of in a logical manner. He didn't want to believe Clavius' theory, but the pieces began to come together when he considered the runner who passed them by the Whirlpool building.

"The runner? I almost forgot him," said Barak.

"What evidence did Barak give you first?" asked Socius, as he let go of the recovered Mortuus.

"The demon," replied Clavius. "Mortuus is the first ever known to have beaten a demon, and I do not mean just to get away from it; Mortuus *destroyed* it, singlehandedly. No human, not one, could have held on to that creature's neck without being annihilated, let alone squeezing it hard enough to stop it from breathing. The demons are very powerful creatures, second only to the Fallen. Restricting its air flow is the only way to destroy it without using magic." Clavius' assistants returned, holding large vials of clear water, and a basket full of very strange looking fruits. Mortuus examined the doorway to the hall. It reminded him of the underground where he had first awoken into this Hell nightmare.

"Drink the water, Mortuus," said Clavius, "It will aide you in your recovery." Mortuus was still dazed from the revelation of his identity and its mystery. "Thank you" he croaked, surprised that his voice had left him. Clavius continued talking.

"Demons are very dense creatures as well. You said that Mortuus was able to hit it and cause it to falter, Barak. Socius, you were struck by the beast. No human could have sent you flying. Luckily you did not have a broken jaw or worse. Yet Mortuus struck the beast, and it fell! No other but one of the Fallen could have caused it such harm." Barak's resistance was giving way as Clavius spoke.

Clavius turned to Mortuus, who had just drunk a vial of the water brought in by the lab assistant.

"Mortuus, do you recall anything of your past? You have been to the first and second waters. Have there been any shadows or feelings of memories…anything at all – which you can remember?" asked Clavius. "Any information, small as it may seem to you, would be helpful."

"I have tried to remember, Clavius. I had a sense of a past while at the first waters. But I could not connect to it. I am only aware that memories exist out of reach. Otherwise, there is nothing," said Mortuus. "Are you certain of my…identity?" he asked tentatively. He had also been grappling with logic and reason. "I mean I was slashed up pretty badly by the demon. I have only healed so quickly by the grace of the waters," he offered almost hopefully.

"Well, let me ask you this Mortuus; when you looked at the demon while he was disguised as the Elder, what did you see?" coaxed Clavius.

"That was different. I saw a man shift into what seemed to be a beast, shift back into a man, then back again." replied Mortuus. "It shifted as the air does, in the Sixth Circle; like the heat above the glowing tombs, constantly distorting the air."

Clavius nodded, satisfied that his theory was fact, and Barak had to acquiesce.

"There you have it, friends. Only a magical being could discern the transformed demon; Mortuus *is* one of the Fallen," stated Clavius definitively.

"Only the Fallen can see through the spell?" asked Socius.

"That is correct."

"Then what was Mortuus doing in that underground dungeon with other Fallen? Why were they all in a deathly sleeping state? Why are the Fallen keeping other Fallen imprisoned and hidden away?" Barak questioned.

"And by what means are they kept asleep?" mused Socius.

"I do not have all the answers, my friends," answered the dwarfish Clavius, "But obviously, Mortuus and the others were kept there in an immobilized state because they were not wanted conscious by the others. Since the Fallen have been banished here, I would imagine that

Mortuus and company fell from the grace of their fellows, and were somehow rendered unconscious to keep them under control. I know they are very upset, and are no doubt searching for Mortuus as we speak."

"Your old friends from the mines had quite a bit of interesting news in that regard," offered Socius.

"Oh?"

"The demons that guarded the sleeping Fallen were replaced with some of the smithy demons. The Fallen were so angry they destroyed their underground workers, and the remaining smithy demons are angry because they have to do extra work with fewer workers."

"They will most likely get a lot more work done since they have less 'friends' to fight with. I bet they increase their quotas considerably," chuckled Clavius.

"They have to. The Fallen are arming the fugitive hunters and sending them out to search for Mortuus," said Barak.

"Threatened, you mean. They are not used to fear," noted Clavius. "This is a good sign."

The assistant with the basket moved closer to Mortuus. He seemed to enjoy watching Mortuus quaffing the large vials of water. He held the basket up, urging Mortuus to take the fruit. Mortuus shyly looked around at the others in the room.

"Yes, Mortuus, eat the fruit. It has medicinal qualities and will speed up your regeneration." said Clavius. Socius and Barak watched as Mortuus inspected the fruit.

"What fruit is this, Clavius?" asked Socius. "I have never seen its like before."

"It is from a special tree, Socius. I was given it when it was a small sapling by the Chronicler, centuries ago. I had Homer try to propagate it, but it was beyond his skill." Clavius looked on proudly as Mortuus tasted his first cautious nibble. The fruit, a light, reddish-green skin, about the size of a large olive, changed to a purple color as Mortuus chewed away. Clavius studied his face, and the others grew quiet. The assistants of Clavius took copious notes. "The tree has only recently begun to fruit, but quite heavily," one of them said.

Mortuus became quite elated, curiously filling with joy inside as he ate. The fruit had a sweet enough flavor, though it was not remarkable, but it caused him to remember a similar feeling from an earlier time. The memory, however, did not connect him to anything more than the remembrance of a familiar feeling. Mortuus stomach had been very tight, yet he had not noticed it until now, as the fruit seemed to settle

his insides and release a stress he had not noticed. He also became

acutely aware of his extreme hunger. Curiously, his back started to itch,

but he could not stop eating until the very last of the fruits was gone.

After, he sat, satisfied, drinking from the vials again and scratching his

back.

"I was very hungry, I did not know how so until I started eating."

enthused Mortuus as the assistants added to their notes, scribbling

excitedly. Just then he caught himself and, embarrassed, looked

sheepishly at the group. "I... am sorry," he stuttered, "I did not mean to

eat all the fruits..."

Clavius and Barak laughed out loud.

"Have no shame, my friend. The fruit was all for you. Socius is

usually the only one who ever gets as hungry, because he is still a

growing boy," smiled the short, stout man, "It was our pleasure, our

pleasure!" Clavius assured him. "Now, I need you to remove your

robes so I can inspect your back, Mortuus."

The assistants eagerly helped to remove the tattered cloth. It was

very light for its thickness. They laid it across one of the tables,

examining the fabric closely, looking through small round glasses that made the fibers much larger to the eye. Mortuus quietly noticed the assistants had a similarity to Clavius, but seemed younger, thinner and taller. He forgot his thoughts as Clavius and Barak moved behind him. Darius, who had been sitting quietly in the corner of the room the whole time, stared at Clavius, waiting for the next revelation.

Clavius scanned the back of Mortuus as Barak and Socius watched curiously. "Ahh – here. Do you all see this?" Clavius pointed to a small area just above the left scapula. "Watch as I press it. Barak, Socius - move back a few more steps."

"I see nothing Clavius." said Socius. "What are you looking pointing at?"

"His wings. They are hidden magically when not in use, but a slight pressure to the proper area and they should open reflexively. Unless an angel wants to use them, they stay concealed. Now watch." Clavius pushed his finger into a spot on Mortuus' back. Mortuus flinched in discomfort for a moment, but did not make any other movement. Suddenly a pair of thin ridges appeared in the skin along Mortuus' backbone, and then the ridges extended into an elongated row of bloody stumps down each side. The stumps then retracted into Mortuus's back quickly, leaving no trace or sign they existed at all.

49

"I suspected this." said Clavius grimly.

"What was that?" asked Darius.

"The Fallen must have been very upset with Mortuus for something. They sawed his wings off, and I would assume those of the others. This is very bad thing for an angel to do to another." Clavius shook his head gravely.

"That row of stumps was what was left of the wings of Mortuus," said Clavius. He was examining the face of Socius, who seemed, in particular, to have been jolted when the wing stubs were revealed. "Socius, are you feeling alright? Looks like I shocked you a bit. Maybe this is too much for a young-"

"I...am fine," replied Socius weakly. "I've seen far worse in the battle games. It just seemed too horrific, even for Hell." Socius looked at Barak and Clavius, who were staring at him with concerned faces. "I am fine!" he insisted. Clavius and Barak knew better. They would take it up with Socius later. One of the assistants jerked around toward Socius, scribbling more notes.

"Socius, Barak – you must take Mortuus to the Chronicler immediately," Clavius advised urgently, and to Mortuus he was reassuring. The Chronicler will help you, Mortuus." He turned to his assistants. "Summon the runner; tell him to get to the society's meeting place near Basel and tell him to say 'there is a theory' as the password when he arrives. They will know what to do. And tell them I have positive confirmation this time."

The assistants left the room hurriedly. Socius handed Mortuus his robe, and they all turned to follow the path of the assistants.

"What did you mean 'this time' Clavius?" asked Socius as they walked out into the large cavern.

"The last time we thought that Hell was near to change," replied Barak.

"We all agreed then, Barak," said Clavius irritated. "Even you."

"I am not denying it." responded Barak.

"What is this theory you two speak of?" asked Socius.

"The theory?" stalled Barak, looking at Clavius with a small amount of caution.

"I believe it will be okay to explain the theory to our friends, Barak," said Clavius. "Would you like to, or should I?" Barak considered a moment.

"I will," said Barak. "This will be brief, however because we need to move again and soon." He stood, pacing as he spoke. "There is a group of people in Limbo that believes we will one day be freed from Hell. Clavius and I are members of that group." Mortuus and Darius stared, unbelieving at what they had just heard. Socius winced. Barak noted their reactions and continued. "The group believes that we will one day befriend a member, or members, of the Fallen, who - I do not need to remind you, but it is important to remember - are the most powerful beings in Hell. Because the Fallen have been exiled from somewhere and it is in their nature to return from whence they came, we feel that they will, in fact, one day do just that…return to wherever it is-"

'Heaven?" injected Darius, incredulous.

"Wherever it is, Darius," said Barak. "Or, the Fallen will find a way to escape from this place.

"Hell?" injected Darius again.

"Wherever this is," returned Barak.

"We know from the logs of Aristotle that Fallen always fly straight upward, passing through the mist, although we do not know what exists beyond. We do expect that there may be much more to Hell than we are aware of." Barak paused and searched the eyes of his ardent listeners.

"Is that it?" asked Mortuus, eager to hear more.

"No," said Barak. "There are many ideas, and many variations, but the generally agreed upon thought is that we will, we must, befriend the Fallen first before any change can occur. This revelation, Mortuus, has just happened, varying slightly - we had not considered that the Fallen would be warring within their own society." Clavius suddenly became animated.

"We can discuss more on this later, Barak, when we arrive at Basel," he urged, "We must leave now!"

"I would like to hear more about the theory while we walk, Clavius," said Darius. Socius and Mortuus nodded in agreement. They all began moving toward the hallway.

"Yes," said Socius, "As would I. I have spoken with you many times, Barak. Why did you not discuss this before?" Socius was slightly miffed.

"Take no offense, Socius," answered Barak. "This was very much a secret to be kept from the Elders. We suspected they were friendly with the demons for some time, and now this has been confirmed. We have merely been waiting for you to get to the proper age -"

"By the Astrochron I am well over six hundred years old, Barak," grumbled Socius, "How old must I be to get to the 'proper' age?"

"Yes, Socius, but you were born and raised here," said Barak, stopping a moment to address Socius directly, "and your life has been a learning experience for us all. According to the laws of Hell that we have observed, you should not have aged at all. Yet you grew older, and now appear as an adolescent. You eat, you sleep because you must. No others require food or drink here Socius. We only eat to feel alive, and sleep so we can dream about our lives and those pleasant memories we once experienced. You, youngling, are another one of Hell's mysteries. It does not matter that you are six hundred years old," Barak smiled as he paused, "you are still an adolescent."

"Everyone, we must go. Now," demanded Clavius. "Mortuus, you and Darius need to put on the new robes Socius brought you." Clavius gestured toward two folded piles of cloth on a nearby table. "These new robes should make it more difficult for anyone to tell you are from the outside. I only hope we have no problems from those who have seen you already."

Clavius, Socius and Barak exited the room as the pair of men dressed quickly and joined them outside the room. As they traveled back through the cavern, Mortuus saw a distant glow of many colors coming from a tunnel under the sloping path that led up to the hallway.

"Clavius," asked Mortuus, "What is that glowing I see?" He pointed to the tunnel.

"That tunnel leads to the tree of the Chronicler," answered Clavius, "And the glow is the tree itself. It is unlike any tree you have ever seen, or will see. I will take you to the tree another time Mortuus, right now we really have to move along."

Mortuus was compelled to stare into the tunnel. For a brief moment, a memory flashed, and then dissipated before Mortuus could grasp its meaning. He recognized the tree, but his memory faded, and was no more.

They continued to the hallway, and to the surface. Mortuus was feeling much better than anytime ever before, but back on the surface of Limbo, he could not help but feel the crushing weight of Hell, which lay just outside the walls.

Chapter 50

The Secret Society of Limbo

The group had been walking for a long time on their way to Basel. Basel was the meeting place of a secret group of the oldest citizenry of Limbo. Whenever irregular occurrences were reported in Hell, this group, who had no ties of friendship with the Elder's Council, would rendezvous. The last meeting had been prompted by the disappearance of the three Elders over a century earlier, and now they were meeting again to discuss the appearance of Mortuus, the only member of the Fallen ever to have befriended Limbo's citizenry. On the way, Barak told them about the history of the society. He had been a member for many centuries.

The Chronicler, the oldest member of Limbo and charismatic teacher of Barak and many other students of Hell, had founded the discrete group, though he rarely attended any of the meetings. Mortuus and Darius learned that the Chronicler was the keeper of the history of Limbo, recorded and copied by his followers, and placed in his own private library. His library was open only to those he personally picked.

He would not allow the Elders to peruse his tomes and though the Council protested loudly, indignantly, it was to no avail. The Chronicler kept his volumes hidden well and according to legend, or perhaps rumor, there were other volumes in this private library, containing non-historic information. This fact was apparently of great interest to Clavius, who began chatting freely.

"I have not seen these volumes; they are said to contain the language and spells of the Angel-folk, the race of the Fallen. I am hoping that he will reveal his volumes as a natural consequence of our having brought you, Mortuus. He has denied me access since I first revealed my interest in angel lore and magic. The information I have heretofore spoken of has been gleaned from many places, and I had even considered traveling to the underground where you were kept comatose for Gods know how long. I wish Aristotle had returned with just one of the tomes in that underground library. Ahh but he was brave for finding you there. I have not been outside of Limbo since my descent into Hell at my death. Before reading that last travel log of Aristotle, I had not considered ever leaving Limbo. Can you imagine? I had only wished to access the collection of the Chronicler. No one knows where the Chronicler obtained these tomes either. Now he is another great mystery of Hell, that one."

"Aristotle has never brought back any books, but I believe he would have if he had the chance," said a gloomy Socius. "He stopped taking notes along the way a long time ago. It was too dangerous to stop and write so he would dictate his journey to me for scribing and placement into the Great Library when he returned. I thought they would have been of interest to the Chronicler, but the Chronicler has not been seen anywhere near the library."

"The Chronicler has read all of Aristotle's travel logs, Socius, and with great interest," contradicted Barak, "Do you think it a coincidence that I was nearby when Mortuus fought the demon Elder? Little goes on without the Chronicler's knowledge. I was at the library copying the last travel log of Aristotle when I heard from other members of the society that you and the warriors had left Limbo. I dispatched a runner to the Chronicler immediately while I waited for your return. We have known for a long time about the problems of the Elders, though not to the extent of there being a transformed demon among them."

"But Mortuus is one of the Fallen," said Socius. "He might be able to beat another."

"Yes. He might be able to overpower another," added Clavius, "And he might not. Mortuus has only recently awakened, and without memory of the incantations and spells used by Fallen, he would be defenseless against their conjuring. Remember, Mortuus and a great roomful of other Fallen were incapacitated by their fellows. These are a most powerful and cruel lot. Fortunately for everyone, the Fallen would not condescend to skulking about in disguise; they use demons and Elder's to do their base work for them."

Suddenly, a loud horn sounded in the distance. Everyone froze in anticipation.

"What was that?" Mortuus finally asked. Clavius had a worried expression on his face.

"We must hurry. The horn was the summoning for Fallen."

"Perhaps it was Minos reporting a fugitive?" said Socius. Barak, in his fear, was agitated with Socius' guess.

"Have you ever heard Minos blow the horn, Socius? No. Something far more serious has occurred. Make haste my friends!" said Barak, breaking into a semi-run. No one needed more prompting.

"We can hide Mortuus in the forest until we hear from the Chronicler. There is a place there made for just such a purpose," Barak spoke in a rush.

It would be some time before they reached the dense wooded area known as the Dark Forest. In the interim, the group, who had slowed their pace to a brisk walk, had passed through a large vineyard, or fields of what appeared to be grapes. The caretaker was a man called Homer, who Barak described as nearly as ancient as the Chronicler, though not as interesting. Homer was working in his fields when the group passed by. Barak waved and shouted a friendly greeting while still walking hurriedly.

Barak explained as they walked that there were many others who helped Homer, some harvesting, others transferring the grapes into a vast vat, and others who would stomp the fruits into juice. The barrels full of juice were stored in small underground caves until fermentation occurred. This spirit was not the only source of fermented beverage in Limbo, but it was known as the finest. According to Barak, Homer had grown interested in making this version of wine long after arriving; when the scientists first announced the developing of fruits in their laboratories. The fruits were not real grapes, but the nearest imitation in

Limbo, and these fruits were far juicier and delicious. Homer had cultivated the variety he was using far beyond that of the scientists. When fully fermented, the wines were very powerfully intoxicating and highly desired, especially by the demon smithies and guardians of the Whirlpool Building. Homer was forced to hide most of his harvests after the beasts had depleted his first few crops.

"So, the demons enjoy a bit of the drink?" inquired Clavius. "I was not aware of this. It would have been a very useful bargaining chip while I was working in the mines, though I do not believe it ideal to be near a demon when it has a belly full of drink. I am certain they would act as the worst angry drunkards." Clavius became quiet, lost in his thoughts.

"They go absolutely mad for Homer's wine," said Barak, searching the face of the introspective Clavius. "My friend, I can almost hear gears grinding when I look at you. Does this mean something to you?"

"Perhaps. I keep notes on the beasts, and this is a very interesting addition. Has anyone seen the creatures in their intoxicated state? I am curious as to the effect upon them," said Clavius.

"No one has reported seeing them in a drunken state yet," said Barak. "As you said, no one would like to be in close range when the beasts become inebriated. Their temperament is volatile in their most sober state."

"Yes, Barak. I would agree." said Clavius. "I am curious though. Do you or Socius know why I went to work in the mines?"

"I recall there was a great deal of chatter about your move to mining. You went from a well known and respected scientist to a miner very quickly. No one understood why, and the only explanation seemed to be that you were just a sort of quirky fellow. That would be the unofficial explanation."

"That would be partly correct, Barak. There is more though. Did you not ever wonder how I know so much about the Angel folk and their spells and incantations?"

"Of course, it did cross my mind, but I am sorry to say, for one reason or another my time has been taken up to the point of distraction, and I was never able to satisfy my curiosity. But you have our attention now, Clavius. Would this not be an appropriate time to fill us in?"

"Very well. It will do me good to enjoy a little boasting," smiled Clavius, who needed no other encouragement. "I left the Hall of Science for a particular reason which I will not disclose lest it distract from my story. I had no idea of what I would do to pass my eternity,

except that my desire to know about the Angel culture has always
dominated my thoughts." The dwarfish man looked up at Mortuus.
"You have no idea what impact your presence has on my heart and
soul, my friend." Clavius looked ahead again. "I was passing the mines,
and, like you, Exaro and Abreo were there, and called out to me. They
asked me to sit and stay a while, and share any news I might have, as
they offered theirs. I learned, during this conversation, that the demons
who claimed a share of the ore from the mines would often converse
with Eruos, the chief of the three miners, on a regular basis. I listened,
interested to know what anyone had to say to demon workers. Eruos, it
turned out, was one of those odd people who can talk to his own worst
enemy safely. Something about him put the beasts at ease, and always
they would tell of the news of their own world. Since the creatures
were the closest to the Fallen, I determined that I might get more
information about the angel folk from them. Soon after this encounter, I
volunteered to work with the three miners."

"The information I gathered was either from eavesdropping on
their conversations with Eruos, or asking them directly myself. Of the
latter, I did very little, I might add. I am not the silver-tongued Eruos,
and the demons' volatility spilled out on me a few times. I had been

warned not to speak to them by Exaro and Abreo, but my desire got the best of me, and I was painfully reminded of my hubris on several occasions. To remedy my inability to query the beasts, I would speak with Eruos before they returned for ore, and he would ask the questions in his particularly pacifying mannerism. Thus, I became educated in much of the culture, lore and magic of the Angel folk."

"So did you not like the mines, Clavius? You went on to create quite an underground terrain of your own," said Socius.

"I created the underground within a few days, if you would believe it, my boy."

"I do not," returned a surprised Socius. "I do not believe it possible at all."

"I do not lie," chuckled Clavius. "I learned well from my work in the mines. By the time I left, I had Eruos convince the demons they would get far more ore by sharing their spells with him. They considered for a while, and after a few more visits to pick up ore, Eruos had been entrusted with a particular spell, useful for mining work. The only setback is that using it drains humans heavily. It is very productive otherwise."

"Amazing!" exclaimed Socius.

"Yes it is Socius. I may teach it to you one day. And there are other spells too, but I want first to see about our theory." They continued walking, and talking along this line of Clavius' Angel folk knowledge, and the time seemed to pass quickly.

Just before arriving in Luton, Darius began to feel unusually insecure. Though he had been washed of the mud and filth of the Vestibule, the odor seemed always present, though no one else seemed to notice. He would have been content to spend his eternity at the rocky oasis of the Vestibule, where he and his two companion fugitives traveled to after escaping the hell flies. Yet here he was, according to Socius, a full-fledged citizen of Limbo. Darius knew if his true identity was discovered, he would be expelled from Limbo as violently as his friends had been captured and mutilated by the demons, and his torment would surely become far more horrific than his sentence in the Vestibule. Now that his new friend had been discovered to be one of the Fallen, his thoughts became doubts, and an underlying anxiety began to eat at him.

He did not belong in this place, this utopian oasis tucked within the walls of Hell. His friends had been captured while he hid, cowering under a rock as they screamed in pain. He did not belong in the company of Angel-kind. This being, who had befriended him, was his better. All of them would see his inferiority eventually, and then he would be cast out, left behind. The reasoning of Darius, the lifelong slave, was lethal and a darkening depression began to overtake him, when just then, his thoughts were broken by Mortuus, who had been walking at his side most of the way.

"You are troubled still, Darius," said Mortuus, "…and it has to do with your feelings of unworthiness to be here?" Darius was astonished, and Clavius focused in on the conversation. Darius, caught, nodded nervously, guiltily. "I do not understand why, but I sense your pain. You are wrong to feel this way, Darius, and you are causing damage to yourself with this mindset. It is guilt, and a kind of faulty thinking that does not serve you. It is much to bear, your burden. But you overload yourself… unnecessarily." Clavius interjected, staring at Mortuus.

"Is this true, Darius? Is Mortuus accurate in his assessment of your dark mood?" asked Clavius. Barak and Socius turned to look at Mortuus and Clavius. The group had stopped.

"To my shame…it is," said Darius quietly. "My life has never been my own. I was a lifelong slave - always the bottom of society - and I cannot seem to feel any other way. I wait for you all to wise up and dismiss me, more so since discovering Mortuus' true identity. I just cannot shake this feeling of impending abandonment."

"You are highly empathic, Mortuus, an excellent ability but not one I had considered present in the Fallen. You can sense the feelings of others. That can be good as long as you are able to separate yourself and keep your boundaries; otherwise you could get swept into their feelings, experiencing emotion that does not belong to you. It is impressive," said Clavius, who turned to address Darius. "Darius, you are no doubt feeling guilty about your fellows, and maybe having guilt about being in Limbo while so many are tormented on the outside. That can only mean you are a truly good man, a man of virtue, and you absolutely belong here. There are many more that seem to have been misplaced by the mirror of Minos, people of considerably low character. *They* never question their placement. I have not determined the mechanism used to decide eternal placement by the mirror, but you have reached Limbo, Darius. And here you shall stay as long as you like."

Darius smiled at this, as did Socius, Barak and Mortuus, who felt the weight lift from Darius. Barak cautioned the group.

"We have to keep moving." Everyone quickly restarted, resuming a quick walking speed as Barak explained places and their route along the way.

"We have been staying near the outer wall for some time. Soon we will enter Luton, another village known for its specialization. It is there the wine is mixed with herbal concoctions. Our best herbal healers reside there, and we will pass through the village on our return trip. All of Limbo will be alerted and looking for anything out of the ordinary soon. We will circumvent Luton so as not to stir curiosities that might bite us later. Keep your eyes searching skyward. If you should notice any movement, dive to the ground and sit as if we have been talking for ages. Try to appear oblivious to the flying demons, as if we are another philosophizing or storytelling group, chatting and not noticing the world around us. You have noticed a few seated groups already during our travels, my friends?" Barak turned toward Mortuus and Darius, who nodded in acknowledgement. They had seen small clusters of people along the path who did not appear to respond to their presence.

"Barak. How far to the Dark Forest?" asked Socius. "I have not been back this way for ages; it seems the vineyards have grown in size."

"The people of Luton have enlarged the vineyards to increase the spirit production. Demand is very high these days," explained Barak.

"Will we get to sample some of the wines, Barak?" asked Darius. "I have not tasted a good wine for some time. In fact, the last time I recalled the scent of wine was on the breath of my master, who whipped me to death in his drunken state. I am sure it was accidental. Slaves were valuable pieces of property, and none were more faithful than I." Mortuus was walking alongside Darius, listening horrified at his tale. "I should be honest, my friends, I was angry at the master for raping a servant girl in front of all of us as a lesson, and as a display of his power; I provoked my beating by goading him, and insulting his honor. It was the only time I stood up for anyone since my early teenage years." Darius waited for judgment from the others, nervously watching as they reacted. Mortuus stared at him, appearing saddened and frustrated, then amazed at what Darius had gone through. He had no words to express his feelings.

"That is some bad exodus from living, Darius." said Socius. "Did you never fight back against this cruel master?"

"Only once. When I was a teenager, my anger was peaked many times, but mostly I did not act out. One day, after a particularly wicked son of the master spit upon me, I slapped him in the face as hard as I could. His shock at being able to be hurt by me was total, and caused him to run, unable to believe what had happened. For my transgression, I was almost beaten to death that day by the master. The house servants begged his mercy, and reminded him of the high cost of slave youths, and saved my life. From then on I promised my saviors, the servants of the house, to never touch the son or act out again, and that I would be obedient. And for reasons I never fathomed, the cruel boy kept his distance ever after."

"Why be born at all," asked Socius, "if such would be your fate?" Mortuus and Barak nodded, and in an attempt to pick up the spirits of the group, Barak answered Darius' original question.

"Of course, my friend, we will get to taste the wines." He winked at Darius, who smiled as he followed.

Luton appeared on the left of the travelers, through trees that grew sparsely in a field of high grass, roughly 100 meters away. They moved between the wall, which separated them from the river Acheron, and the trees. The path turned toward the outer wall halfway as they came upon the path into the Dark Forest.

There, in the Dark Forest, trees grew tall and stood tightly together. The wood smelled of musty, damp earth, and the trees seemed as serene gods in a state of deep sleep. The path was winding and narrow, and visibility was limited. The forest had meager lighting, only enough to portray a late twilight. It was a beautiful and ominous arrangement.

When they had gone a far distance past Luton, the trail suddenly opened out into a huge lake, circled tightly by trees. Few narrow openings between the trees could be seen, and where they stood looked to be the main entrance to the water's edge. The water was dark, reflecting the forest that surrounded it. Mortuus gazed intently; he could see a shimmering dance of colors across the surface that phased in and out of his vision.

"What are those waves of color across the surface?" he asked. The group looked at the body of water, then at Mortuus questioningly.

"Where do you mean, Mortuus?" asked Barak. "I do not see what you speak of." Mortuus looked at Barak.

"There. Toward the center," Mortuus pointed.

Socius winced as he looked at the water, not sure of what he saw. Darius looked and shook his head.

"I see nothing but the dark lake, Mortuus," answered Socius.

"As do I," said Barak. "Clavius?"

"Aye," replied Clavius. "Just water. Perhaps you are weary, Mortuus. We have traveled a great distance, almost a quarter circle since leaving my cottage in Porto."

But Mortuus looked again, sure of what he had seen. The colors were still present; fading a bit, then suddenly appearing brightly and plainly in his sight.

"I am tired, though I still see the colors. Can we stop here for a few minutes?" asked Mortuus. Barak, addressing Mortuus and Darius, spoke.

"Actually, that was our intention, Mortuus. My friends, I would ask that you step into the lake. For you Mortuus, this water will begin to regenerate the magical power within, restoring that which was lost or stolen by the Fallen's spells and the foul liquid they fed you to keep you unaware and forgetting." Mortuus looked puzzled, but seemed to understand why he was seeing the colors on the lake, as they wavered in and out – it was the magic, the same magical power he had seen concealing the demon Elder. What did this lake conceal, he wondered, or was it only the signature of magic? Darius began to remove his robes.

"Will this water do anything for me?" asked Darius. Clavius smiled, as did Barak.

"You will no longer smell even the faintest scent of outer Hell." said Clavius. "And you will feel invigorated even more so than when you drank from the Second Waters." Mortuus was staring at the surface, looking down to see the bottom. He could see nothing but blackness.

"Mortuus. Please, enter the water. We need to hide in the trees again soon. They will be coming soon for you and I want your angel healing to begin promptly. You will be much more useful at your strongest, both magically and physically. When you two finish, we will move quickly to our rendezvous point. Luckily, we do not have to go all the way to Basel. In fact, we need to backtrack a bit."

"Where is this meeting, Barak? I understood it to be *in* Basel." said Socius.

"You'll see." said Barak. "Now jump in – I know it is cold Mortuus!" he yelled to the shivering angel. "Darius – there you go!" And both were in the water, underneath, then up, gasping for breath as the shock of the coldness of the water convulsed their bodies. "Feels good, does it not?" Mortuus looked at Barak as if he were crazy. "Very well. Now, both of you out. We need to go."

Soon, the group was walking along the path, back through the thick, dark forest. Just as Socius was about to ask Barak how much further, they came to a sharp turn, past a large boulder that was on their right when they came this way earlier. Barak stopped them all with a silent wave of his hand, then, looking at the large boulder, he spoke. The words were familiar to Mortuus, but he did not know why.

"*Gahdtwer!*" said Barak directly to the stone face. The boulder rolled slowly out onto the path as Barak moved back. A small passage hole in the forest was revealed behind where the boulder had been, a crawlspace carved through the thick tree bottoms. It was not high enough for anyone to stand upright, and so Barak motioned to the group to get on all fours and crawl. When they had passed him, he backed in on his hands and knees, then spoke again to the rock face. He scampered into the hole and caught up to the group. The blunt sound of the boulder rolling back into place followed his movements.

"Are you okay, Barak?" asked Clavius. "I could have cast the spell."

"I am fine, Clavius." replied Barak. "Just a bit weak. I have felt worse." Mortuus was puzzled by this exchange, as were Darius and Socius.

"Did something happen? Clavius, why did-" Mortuus was cut off by Clavius.

"It was the spell, Mortuus. Perhaps we should have let you practice your art. Magic use by humans causes severe energy drain. We do get better with practice. It takes so long to get our energy back after a heavy spell like moving that boulder. The long hallway under my hut incapacitated me for a week. The bigger the job, the bigger the energy drain."

"You learned the magic spell from the smithy demons?" asked Socius.

"That one I learned from the Chronicler," said Clavius. "All the members know of it. Tell no one of this, Socius, not even your dearest friends. One member of the society used the spell publicly and was reported to the Elder's Council by a so-called friend. He mysteriously disappeared soon after. Now that we know the Elder's are in league with the demons, I correctly assume my old friend is suffering in outer Hell."

"I must rest, friends." said a weakened Barak. "I will catch up with you."

"Enough about the magic." said Clavius. "We are almost there and my knees are getting raw; pretend as if you did not hear the spell word when we are in front of the others."

The group crawled for a short time, taking in the ornate carving along the way. The trees had been etched carefully all through the path. Then a circular, hollowed rock had been wedged into the hole, like an earring, to keep the trees from growing back together. Barak explained that the trees healed up quite fast; that was how so much wood could be found in Limbo. As long as the trees were not fully cut down they would regenerate, just like humans, and keep up the supply of wood for Limbo's usage. This stand of trees hid the group and any others who ventured through. No one else knew of the passage except for the society, who had used it for meetings for millennia. The only other way in or out was to fly, but the space was camouflaged very well by the canopy of the treetops. They crawled until they reached a small trickle of a stream that flowed toward the dark lake, where another path opened up. They stood up, relieved, as the roughness of the tree roots and gravel on their knee caps was gone. A thin path took them to a small, rocky mound. Barak caught up just as they arrived.

"*Gahtwer Viatra!*" whispered Clavius. A second later, the mound opened wide and revealed a rocky stairwell. The opening was large enough to easily walk in, single file. They stepped downward, and a set of torches flamed up as they walked near, surprising Mortuus and Darius. They were in a large room again, not unlike the cavern which led to Clavius' work area, though not as grand. The meeting was held in a corner of the cavern. There were eight people already seated around a long, flat table of stone, each of them studying Mortuus intently, staring as if none of the others of the group were present. Mortuus, uncomfortable at their scrutinizing, stared back at each of them.

"So much for tact and grace," said an irritated Clavius. "Please do not stare at Mortuus; he is *very* sensitive, and your staring is *very* rude." Clavius berated his fellow members for their lack of consideration. "Mortuus, Darius and Socius - please sit here." He pointed to the empty far end of the table. "You are our guests, and get the good seats. Do not mind their rudeness, Mortuus. They have never seen your kind before."

"When will the Chronicler arrive, Percival?" asked Barak of one of the members. He waited for an answer, and then studied the eyes of Percival, who was still gawking at Mortuus. "Well? No answer?" Barak was getting impatient.

"Barak, I think Percival has bad news," answered a frustrated Clavius. "Percival, speak already." Percival, looking quite stunned, began to speak, though he stammered at first. The other society members stopped staring at Mortuus, and turned toward Barak and Clavius while Percival answered, though occasionally shot glances randomly at the newly awakened member of the Fallen.

"There is a great disturbance, Barak. This angel...pardon me... Mortuus, is known to be missing from the custody of the Fallen. Their high demons have been to the Elders, and some have inquired as to the whereabouts of Morpheus." Mortuus began to tighten up, fear gripping him in a cold vise. Percival continued, "I do not know if you heard it, but-"

"Yes. We all heard the horn," interrupted Barak. His face was pasted with worry and irritation. "Back to my original question. What about the Chronicler, Percival? Is he coming or not?"

"The Chronicler has been made aware, Barak. You know how he is – no one can predict what he is up to, but I suspect he will not appear, as usual. The demons will visit him first when the Elders have no answers. There are guards who work for the Elders without questioning their commands, and I am certain they will be dispatched to find… answers." Percival looked at Mortuus and Darius with worry and unexpectedly cut to the chase. "The strangers will have to leave," he sputtered.

"Wait!" roared Clavius, 'What of the theory? This is not part of it, Percival, damn you!"

"The theory is vague, Clavius. What makes you think it would really manifest?" argued a predictably defensive Percival. "We have had this discussion many times-"

"That is your opinion only, Percival. We have a great chance if we can only grab it by the reins. Our fear is all that keeps us from realizing our dream." said a red faced Clavius.

"*Our* dream, Clavius?" asked another society member seated next to Percival.

"Is it not our reason for meeting all these millennia, Justinius?" asked Clavius. "Why do we gather at all? Do you not recall our original intention? Or are we some snobbish social club with a foolish wish list!" Clavius was yelling.

"We meet to keep abreast of news and the happenings in Limbo, Clavius." replied a worried Justinius. "This is to our mutual benefit. Were it not for the Elders, we would have great chaos in –"

"The Elders?" asked Socius. "The Elders? The Elders who allowed the demons into their ranks? The Elders? Are you insane?!! Since when did we trust those pompous old fools?"

"I do not care for your tone, Socius." said Percival sharply. "The times are too dangerous for secret schemes and foolish uprisings. The angel and the fugitive have to leave before we are persecuted along with them!" Percival's desperation was growing more apparent. He turned toward Mortuus, whose face had softened into a deeply hurt sadness. Darius began to stare downward, sighing, and Mortuus closed his eyes.

"I am very sorry. I realize you have come through much pain and trouble. Of course it is for the safety of the whole -"

"Say no more Mortuus - you will stay, the sycophants can leave and hide their cowardly faces in their Elder friend's robes!" Socius was livid.

"Mortuus, Darius and Socius – please wait for us outside," interrupted Clavius loudly as he stared directly into the face of Percival. "We will not be long. Barak and I must confer with our *fellows*."

The three left the cavern while the society members began a shouting match. The three sat outside the rocky mound, each stunned or angry and contemplating their next steps. Mortuus thought about how he would miss Limbo. Nothing good existed in outer Hell; even the rocky oasis in the Vestibule could not touch the experience of Limbo. He thought about his healing and if that would continue in outer Hell, now that he would be without the waters and fruits. His thoughts went to the revelations that he was an angel and just what it would mean outside these walls. Could he fight throughout Hell? And what would happen if he was captured by the Fallen, who had cruelly cut his wings off? They would surely return him to that place he had awoken from, erasing his memories and removing the magical energies that were renewing within him. If he had just had more time...

Clavius and Barak emerged from the rocky underground. They looked disheveled and beaten, worn out from their arguing and frustration.

"The news is grim," reported a somber Barak. "I would speak to you when I have calmed down, my friends. For now we will turn back on our path and get away from these fools I had mistaken for friends."

Quietly, the group walked, and then crawled back the way they had come into the secret meeting area. Gloomily, they avoided Luton, on their right this time, and passed the vineyards of Homer much later. The demons would be searching in the inhabited places for the fugitives; Percival, Justinius and the other members of the society had informed Clavius and Barak that the guards were in fact looking for two persons who had entered Limbo, not just Mortuus, although he was the higher priority and thus in the greatest danger.

Clavius was shocked at the attitude of the society when he had ultimately proven the theory of change and how it would come to Limbo. The long talked about and speculated change was the object of conversation for many centuries of society meetings, and now that it was really here, the society was suddenly grim and fearful, obedient to the Elder's Council. All Clavius could think of was how badly he had misjudged his friends. The long walk was silent until Barak finally spoke.

"My friends, I am in grave pain over the society's decision to expel you. We are going to return to Bremen, despite the judgment of my fellow society members, and seek answers from the senior scientist Benjamin, who we met with earlier. Benjamin is about the wisest person I know besides the Chronicler, and who I trust the most. Militus will send runners past us if there is news we should be aware of. I look upon your faces, I see pain and fear. Know this; we have no intention of expelling either of you; do not fear. You are among friends."

Mortuus and Darius half smiled, happy for this support from Barak, but uncertain if they should hope. Both knew their presence was causing a great disturbance in Limbo, and though they were safe within the walls, always there was the knowledge of Hell outside that played in the background of their awareness.

"Why do you give them false hope, Barak, when we are being watched even now by the society members?" Clavius was suddenly cynical. Mortuus watched as the sad, dwarfish man spewed out his pain in the form of negativity. Barak angered and shouted back his reply.

"Clavius! Fool! I am not expelling anyone. This IS part of the theory. We cannot destroy our one alliance with a real member of the Fallen! They will find him and place him into the deep sleep again."

"We do not have a choice!" yelled Clavius. "I want the alliance too, Barak, but we have no say in the matter."

"No. We do not seem to." said Barak. "But until we find out, we should not expel them. Let the society complain. Will they report to the Elders? I do not think so."

"Barak," said Clavius. "Gather your wits. Justinius is in favor of the Elders. The society has already been compromised. Can you not see that? The society is infiltrated. How long do you think it will be before the demons disguise themselves as society members? Justinius was the strongest proponent of the theory, yet he has sided fully with the Elder's Council. And I had spoken with him not so long ago…" Clavius trailed off, disheartened, as Barak hung his head sadly.

"This is so wrong," whispered Barak gloomily. "So wrong…"

The group continued walking, saddened, angry, and confused. Mortuus, considering that this would be the last part of his visit to Limbo, studied his surroundings, taking in as many details as possible for his own memories, as if it were the last time he would ever see such sights again. Darius wept to himself quietly, briefly, a sudden knowing overtaking him.

"They will be waiting for us outside the gate," he said. "Just like Aristotle. They must have ambushed him as he left. That Elder, Alcander, knew it would happen. Now they will wait for us."

Concern spread on the faces of the group. Darius was correct. Socius recalled his last meeting with Aristotle, and the feeling of being watched from atop the inner wall. It made sense to him. Clavius growled angrily at the treachery of the Elders, and Barak suddenly became hopeful.

"We would not send you out until it was safe to do so, and I will do all in my power to insure we do not have to part," exclaimed Barak. "Socius, you could send a party of your warrior friends out to ascertain the path is safe, as you did when you found them."

"Against a force of demons, Barak? Aristotle was adept at protecting himself against the imps, and yet still almost lost a few times," cautioned Clavius. "I'm sure one demon is enough, though I would bet the Fallen will use more." Barak grimaced at his blundered thinking; he was trying too desperately to overcome this very unpleasant situation, and obviously losing his battle.

Socius nodded in agreement with Clavius a fraction of a moment before he hit upon a way that the wanted pair could leave safely. He

85

considered this as they walked toward Bremen. If Mortuus and Darius had to return to outer Hell, they could elude the demons waiting outside the gate by taking another passage that Socius had learned of long ago. He had almost completely forgotten about this passage as there had simply been no reason to use it in hundreds of years. Smiling to himself, he walked and planned, but did not bring up his thoughts yet to either fugitive. He would see to it the pathway still existed. Denying the demon fugitive hunters their prey would be his greatest revenge for what they did to his teacher, his friend, and his father.

Chapter 51

The Final Judgment

It was my turn for judgment. I stood outside the doorway of the room, dreading what was to come next. Inside, the centaur and the great, large man were talking in their booming, powerful voices, almost arguing, though in my haze of fear I could not give their conversation my full attention. The last person in front of me had gone inside a few moments before, and I was standing by the entrance trying to seek some escape from my predicament.

The line behind me had stopped queuing not too far back, and the other passenger in the boat, the man who I hated for causing Charon to strike me had begun crying again. I was weakened, and I could not pull together enough energy to hate his weeping. At this point, hate was a waste of energy I could not afford; and I was crying too, the wetness running all over my face, lips and chin. I could not stop it no matter how I tried. It was uncontrollable, like when I first experienced death at my grandfather's viewing.

I was a young boy, age eleven. My mother, stepfather and brothers all went to the funeral home. I was not expecting to cry, and yet as soon as I saw my grandfather's body laid out in the coffin, I lost it. Completely. No one else was affected, it seemed, but me. It was uncontrollable, and for my young self, rather disconcerting. Now I was here, in Hell, and would never see anybody I loved again, and I would suffer permanently, and not know why. There was no way out, no legality, no one to feel pity, and pull me out, no nothing. Period.

Just then, the loudest, most deadly roar came to my ears, and I stopped.

"NEXT!" yelled the voice of the great man. My wits came back to me and I stood tall. I would go with dignity; somehow I would find the will to carry myself through. I had never had a feeling so strongly, and I was not sure why the first time it would occur would be in Hell. I began to breathe in, the foul air passing through my nostrils and into my lungs, but I refused to gag. Instead, I ignored this 'flavor' of Hell and became calm. I closed my eyes and breathed deeply, and searched within myself for a space of peace. I would remember my life one last time, as positively as I could, and hold my memories as best I could. I entered the room of my final judgment, and I embraced my lifetime as I walked toward the mirror.

The centaur was much larger close up, as was the great man. They were conversing as if I was a passing leaf on the wind, and that was fine with me. I walked straight up to the mirror, a door-sized silver slab set in an ornately carved metal piece that looked like it was solid gold. But I was not interested in anything but my reflection, and as I strived for peace within, I watched as my entire life unfolded in the reflection.

Chapter 52

The Newcomer's Arrival

Mortuus saw a bright light ahead, just through the trees on the group's left. A line of light had appeared from out of nowhere, splitting reality from the misty ceiling to the ground just behind the trees for a single moment, yet no one else seemed to notice it; everyone continued the hurried pace, walking as if nothing had happened. Mortuus stopped and struggled to see through the trees, to view the ground where the light had touched. Something was there, but he could not quite get his eyes on it. It was hidden just out of sight. Darius had noticed Mortuus' had stopped and saw his erratic head movements. He looked also in the direction of his friend, and saw what Mortuus could not. He turned back to Mortuus.

"What are you looking for?"

"There is something there, behind the trees, but I cannot see it. Can you see it?" asked Mortuus.

"Yes." replied Darius. "It is only a man; he appears to be a newcomer by his dress. I say this because everyone in Limbo wears fine robes, like ours."

"I must see. Come with me. I want to see this newcomer." Darius saw that the others had kept their pace and were disappearing as the path curved ahead. They had not noticed the trailing pair had stopped. "We'll catch up," continued Mortuus, "I am in no hurry to leave. Did you see the strangely beautiful light Darius?"

"No. I did not." said Darius, "but I thought I detected the scent of outer Hell for a split second. It passed so quickly, I am wondering if I really smelled it."

"Yes - I also caught that scent. I must see what caused it."

Darius was happy to follow Mortuus, like when they first met. This time they walked through the dense forest in the direction of where he had seen the newcomer. The newcomer had silently stepped behind a tree ahead, but was still partially visible. He appeared to be hiding, but from whom wondered Darius. Mortuus was ahead and now seeing a lot more than Darius. The strange newcomer was poorly hidden, looking around, with a puzzled expression on his face, but his body was surrounded by a sparkling field of energy that only Mortuus could see.

The light was fading slowly from his vision as Mortuus cautiously approached. The newcomer, seeing the large presence of the angel, stared fearfully, not sure what to do or think. He searched the forest, checking for a quick escape route. Mortuus, sensing the fearful man's desire to flee, stopped and motioned to Darius to stop behind him.

"Wait, please friend, I would speak with you only a few moments, if you are willing." The newcomer stood silently for a second, then relieved, beckoned to Mortuus. Mortuus moved closer, watching as the last of the sparkling light faded. Darius followed on the heels of his Angel friend.

"I do not know where I am. Or who you are," said the stranger, scanning Mortuus and Darius.

"You have been sentenced to Limbo, my friend. Where were you last?" asked Mortuus.

"I stood in the room of the hall, where I was before a large mirror."

"And when did you arrive here?"

"Just now. I just arrived here. This is Limbo? Are you sure?" The man was searching the eyes of Mortuus, trying to discern that he was real and of a peaceful nature.

"Yes. You have been given the lightest sentence in Hell." The man heaved a sigh of relief as Mortuus said this. Swooning, he fell back into a nearby tree, knocking his head. He stood up, holding the back of his head, but still he smiled as he cursed under his breath. It was clear the man knew just how lucky he was. Mortuus now recognized the colorful light he had seen was the magic of the mirror teleporting the newcomer.

"I have been transported to Limbo then?" said the happy newcomer, his spirits rising. "Where do I go first?"

"You seem to need new robes, my friend," said Mortuus. The angel was feeling he and Darius needed to return to the path; their friends would be searching for them. Before Mortuus had seen the beautiful light, the group had passed Porto and were approximately half way between Porto and Terni, an easy walk for the newcomer. Mortuus offered his help to the stranger. "You may follow us back to the path, and we will point you toward Porto where the robe makers will dress you as finely as we are." Mortuus said this as he turned to display the fine craftsmanship of his robes; Darius also turned to offer a view of his. The newcomer looked at the pair's dress robes, a strange look on his face.

"So…they don't have jeans here then?"

Chapter 53

Demon Attack

Mortuus saw it first – a projectile moving so fast toward the group that it defied all that they knew. No bird had flown so fast nor creature moved so quickly that they could not follow, yet it was coming at them, a blur of movement. Clavius and Barak did not see it, nor did Darius. Mortuus yelled loudly to alert them, but only Socius acknowledged seeing the creature moving toward them. It was a huge man shape with giant-wide wings. When it neared them, it turned its body upward and stopped in the air, then dropped to the ground. Its wings vanished, and the creature stood before the stunned and terrified group. It was a demon, only it was more like a human than the Morpheus demon who Mortuus had beaten. It had the distorted features of a demon, but it looked like a cross between each. They were being attacked by a high demon.

"*B'rithjall – mahe!*" spoke the creature suddenly, in a hissing voice. Everyone, including Mortuus, could feel their joints stiffening up, the legs and arms frozen, all movement inhibited. They could not even speak. It had cast a spell that paralyzed them. Even Mortuus could not fight this beast.

The demon stared at Mortuus and approached, throwing him to the ground roughly. The beast turned Mortuus face down and tore his robes enough to bare his full back, speaking a strange spell as it did so. Mortuus felt a familiar twinge along his back that he first felt in the laboratory of Clavius – his wings had opened, or what were supposed to be his wings. The group saw for the second time the elongated rows of bloody stumps that had once been full wings. The demon angrily kicked Mortuus in his ribcage, sending the angel on his side in pain, and unable to move even to hold his pained ribs. The demon cursed him even as he rained down abuse, fueled by his rage.

"Worthless, filthy creature," spewed the violent demon. "Hiding among these simple children!" Several kicks struck the helpless angel-fugitive. He was on the ground cringing in pain as his ribs cracked, the paralysis disabling any protective movement. "You will wish you had remained asleep!" A kick to the face smashed his nose and it erupted with blood. "Superior, angel?"

Socius, watching his friend at the mercy of this giant beast, grew red in the face, and felt his body begin to loosen up – he was able to move again. He looked around at the others, still motionless. The demon landed another kick in the legs of Mortuus as Socius got up and approached from behind. "I think not!" The demon, sensing Socius, backhanded him with barely an effort, sending him flying into a tree ten meters away, and then resumed his violence on Mortuus. Socius lay still against the tree.

The demon, tiring of his abuse of Mortuus, reached into a sash around his waist, pulling out a long metallic horn tucked there. It walked over toward Socius nonchalantly, and readied to blow the horn as it kicked the youth against the tree. The hand that held the metal horn, which had been in the process of raising the horn to its mouth, was pinned into its throat as an arrow abruptly appeared to grow out of it. Its face was a question, not understanding what had happened. Another projectile followed, penetrating the right side of the demon. The creature fell to the ground, writhing in pain and anger as it had never before, the impertinence of violence against it seeming more to fuel its rage than even the pain of the shafts impaling it. As the group, who had been paralyzed in place, watched, a small company of fifteen heavily armed warriors suddenly surrounded the fallen demon, followed by a giant centaur, its crossbow firing into the demon as it scanned the furious, pained creature.

The soldiers, who had a range of weapons from spears to maces and long bows, and swords, jabbed at the demon, stabbing or smashing any body part exposed. The demon turned over, rolling to its left onto its belly, and the warriors who stood nearest it were suddenly flying away, as wide wings appeared from nowhere. The remaining warriors yelled to stay back, as the centaur shot bolt after bolt into the wings, pinning the beast to the ground like some macabre butterfly. The warriors stayed out of the way, striking, slicing and stabbing the demon at any sign of movement.

The soldiers kicked the horn out of the creature's pinned hand. The centaur walked up close, clearing the men from the area, before addressing the demon. It looked up at the centaur, with fear in its eyes for the first time in its existence. The centaur spoke in a soft and strange language, not the common tongue of Hell, and before everyone's eyes, the beast became smoke. The demon was destroyed.

Mortuus, still laying in pain, began to be able to move again, but he was in too much pain to get up. The warriors helped him up gingerly as he had some broken ribs. Socius was also brought to his feet by the warriors, who mostly turned out to be his friends; Socius also thought he knew who this great centaur was from Aristotle's descriptions. Barak and Clavius were in a state of joy, as was Darius. The spell soon wore off fully, and they met their saviors and this greatest of warriors, the Master Centaur, Chiron.

The friends of Socius, his warrior playmates with whom he had trained and combated with in the battle games, were happy to see and save their long time friend. And they were happy beyond belief to have fought a greater demon alongside the greatest of warriors, Chiron. The Master Centaur had been searching for Socius, and wanted to meet Mortuus. The warriors, who had proudly escorted Chiron, told him along the way of the arrival of Mortuus and the subsequent demon slaying.

Coming up from the back of the crowd of warriors was Militus, newly arrived on the scene. The warriors, who were buzzing in the joy and excitement of this great adventure, surrounded Militus, telling him of their hand in the destroying of the demon, their fighting alongside Chiron. Militus walked toward the wounded warriors who had been thrown aside by the mighty wing opening of the beast, seeing that they were tended to before moving toward Chiron, who was retrieving his arrows from the kill site. Mortuus was held up by Darius and Socius as he rubbed his ribs and gently touched his battered face; he was already regenerating, his ribs were very sore, but no longer broken from the violent kicks.

Militus, with serious face, gave Socius a note, passed on, he said, from Benjamin. Socius took it, reading it quietly, and his disdain apparent. The youth then handed it to Barak, who read and passed it to Clavius, who read it aloud – his tone was defeated.

My friends – danger is coming. You must leave by another way. I know the predicament the society has put you in. Get to the mine. Chiron will take you back to his circle until danger has passed.

Benjamin

Mortuus winced as he suddenly touched his sore nose too roughly, and Darius shoulders sunk as his head fell to his chest. Their fears were truly confirmed; they would be exiting Limbo, returning back to outer Hell. They had feared this all along, sensing it within, but allowed hope at the prior words of Barak. Clavius frowned. Now it was a certainty.

The joy left the air around the odd fugitive pair. Socius wore his disappointment clearly; his countenance was sadness.

"Militus – what have you done with Alcander?" asked Socius. The Elder was not with the group, as Socius had suspected he would not be.

"He is being detained, silently, until the demons leave. They have gone to search from the other end of Limbo. The Chronicler will be getting a visit if he has not already met them." Militus looked very serious. "I would introduce you all formally. And I want you to know this is a very old friend of mine." Militus pointed in the direction of the Master Centaur. "My friends, this is Chiron." The centaur stared at each person, bowing respectfully and causing slight discomfort with the natural intensity of his stare. Mortuus seemed to understand the centaur protocol, and bowed back, as best as he could while rubbing his ribs again. Chiron stared for a full minute at Darius, who squirmed and did not follow Mortuus' lead. Finally Socius nudged him with his elbow, and whispered for him to bow his head politely. Socius knew the protocol well as he had copied it into the logs of Aristotle. Darius nervously bowed, and Chiron moved through the rest of the group. Darius sighed loudly in relief as Socius chuckled.

"My friend," said Militus to the towering centaur, "These are the two who have visited us recently." Militus gestured to Mortuus. "This is Mortuus, of whom Phlegyas spoke to you, recently awoken by Aristotle. He does not know of his origins, or history or even what his real name is. Aristotle provided him with the equipment and a name to pass through to Limbo, although it was still quite challenging."

"I am aware of the challenges of traveling through Hell, Militus. My own wounds are not fully healed, even with your waters and elixirs." Chiron examined Mortuus, studying him as if no other thing in Hell existed. Suddenly, he stopped looking, though his eyes were open and staring widely into open space. Militus knew what was happening, though he had not seen it for so very long. Mortuus, confused, started to speak to Chiron as if trying to snap him out of his trance; Militus' hands flew up immediately, to silence Mortuus and all the others. Chiron was in one of his trances.

Chiron was back on the ice, the same ice as in his prior vision. Eight Fallen were before him, and their demons growled and snarled. He could see his centaur herds, and within their ranks were warrior humans, armed heavily. There was something in the freezing, windy air overhead, something that Chiron strained to see...

Then it was over. Chiron was back, confused momentarily, with the entire group watching, staring at him. Some of the warriors had joined the group and were looking at the dazed centaur. Militus watched and waited.

"Are you alright, my friend?" asked Militus.

"I am fine. Do you remember my inner visions?" asked Chiron. Militus nodded. "Well," said Chiron, "Even in Hell I have them. We had so much to talk of I did not get a chance to discuss them with you yet." Now Chiron looked at the group of four. "You are one of the Fallen, Mortuus. Why did you not fly at the creature when it attacked your group?"

"I was paralyzed by the beast's incantation, as were we all. But even if we were not so immobilized, I have no wings," replied Mortuus sadly.

"No wings?" Chiron was stunned. "What happened to your wings?"

"They were removed by those who imprisoned me in the sleep," said Mortuus.

"Removed?" Something was not right, but Chiron would not venture to guess. It was a time of urgency for them all.

102

"Sawed off," offered Clavius. Chiron considered, disbelief pasted on his face, and felt much sympathy for Mortuus. He was aware of the cruelty with which such an act must be perpetrated, and he sensed no disdain or the grand hatred that he usually felt in the presence of Fallen. In fact, he experienced Mortuus as quite the opposite, a gentle being, but with a strength perhaps even the angel himself was unaware of.

"This demon was far more dangerous than Morpheus. It was terrifying," said Mortuus.

"Until your strength rebuilds, I would recommend you avoiding any direct confrontations with demons. It was luck that the demon, disguised as the Elder, was weaker. That may be why he was assigned to infiltrate the Elders Council. You might be in very different circumstances had this been your first encountered demon." said Clavius. Mortuus nodded in agreement as Chiron studied the disabled fugitive Fallen. Chiron generally disliked angel folk – the Fallen had tasked him and his kind as workers in Hell for eternity. Yet somehow, he liked this angel Mortuus, and he would learn more before making any judgment. Militus waved to get Chiron's attention, calling him toward Socius.

"Master Chiron, here is the person you have sought since coming here. Socius, you have been told of Chiron by Aristotle?" asked Militus. Socius was wide-eyed, excitement brimming. He was finally meeting the head of the centaurs, the fabled Chiron himself, subject of many lessons from his various teachers. He smiled widely.

"Yes – I thought I would never get to meet you," said Socius. "Yet, I would prefer that circumstances were better for our meeting. You have heard of the misfortune of my teacher?"

"Yes." The centaur was abrupt. "That is my purpose for coming here." Socius, curiosity peaked, focused intently on Chiron. "Aristotle was spotted near my post, in a cave that is forbidden to all centaur folk by the Fallen. The cave has watchers standing outside, ready to sound off should anyone approach the entrance; I suspect there is a horn to summon the Fallen in their inventory. My commanders informed me that your teacher, Aristotle, has been taken inside the cave. It is most, most unfortunate. This cave is where the Fallen hide special prisoners, whom they personally torment, though on very rare occasions. We do not know why, nor do we know how or where they caught Aristotle. It is my belief that-"

"Alcander and the demon Elder betrayed Aristotle!" interrupted the bitterly angry Socius with a shout. Chiron was taken aback by the young man's rage and contempt; Socius put out a great deal of power in his outburst. "They work with the demons and Fallen, the Elders betray-"

"Whoa! Easy does it Socius," said Militus sternly. "You are among friends here." The whole group, with a few of the warriors who were now standing around, stared at the enraged young man. They watched and waited for Socius to calm down, and when he finally did, tears began to flow from his eyes.

"I am sorry, Master Chiron," said a wet-faced Socius. "I am not well myself; I get enraged and saddened easily, much more so since losing Aristotle. I did not mean to interrupt you, or to be disrespectful. Aristotle spoke very highly of you, and I would have you know I also regard you highly. Forgive my temperament - please continue."

"No forgiveness is necessary, young ward of Aristotle. I am not annoyed by your emotional outburst. Aristotle is missed by all, and I would hope the most by the one he considered as his own son, whom he expressed great pride in." Socius choked and sputtered a moment, as Militus and Clavius smiled. Darius wiped back a quick tear. Chiron paused and looked around at the group that was now standing around, staring, watching and waiting; most of the warriors were there, waiting on Chiron's words, their faces full of compassion for their saddened friend Socius. "I journeyed to Limbo to find out what was happening. This is a strange event for Hell. I learned that Aristotle had freed a member of the Fallen, related to me by Phlegyas, oarsman of the Styx, but I did not know that you had the angel in your midst until I arrived at the gate. The situation requires more serious action, and thus I have decided, not lightly, what must be done." Chiron paused for a few moments. "I am going to rescue Aristotle, Socius. Angel Mortuus, I would ask your help. No others have defeated a demon barehanded. We will not be alone in this risky undertaking. Your human friend from the First Circle will be of no use, however, in our extraction of Aristotle." Chiron looked at Darius, who shrank timidly under the powerful gaze. "But you will stay protected by a few of my fellow centaurs."

Socius could not believe his ears; the warriors were silent, some wishing for the adventure of real battle, but none actually willing to leave Limbo or combat the Fallen. Clavius and Barak stared in disbelief. Socius was ecstatic. Militus' thoughts were also racing, questioning, strategizing.

"How will you face the Fallen?" asked Militus. "That demon was only a fraction of what a Fallen will be. You will end up trapped and tormented alongside Aristotle."

"The Fallen do not frequent the cave," said Chiron, "And as far as they know, Aristotle has been captured and imprisoned there, left to the attentions of their demon workers. I will bide my time, and study their patterns of visitation. Before I made this journey, I could only dream of rescuing Aristotle. But there were signs laid out for me, signs I cannot ignore."

"I met and conversed with Asterion, known to many of you as the Minotaur." The warriors gasped in unison at this. "The Minotaur, Asterion, may be accompanying us if he can get down into my circle. Another sign occurred as Phlegyas spoke to me of you, Mortuus. But alone, even that would not be enough. The ferryman of Acheron, Charon, is missing. His craft was found empty on the landing of the Limbo side of Acheron. This I saw for myself." Mortuus and Darius looked at each other like guilty children as the leader of the centaur kind spoke of Charon.

"Master Chiron," interrupted Darius. "I can tell you what happened to the ferryman." Darius did, and the entire party watched as the usually serious and well composed Chiron displayed stunned disbelief. By the end, the centaur was smiling at Mortuus and Darius.

"So, there is more to you than meets the eye, Darius. By sacrificing yourself, you saved Mortuus and in turn have rid Hell of the menace of Charon. Another sign I cannot ignore." Chiron continued, "Upon entering Limbo, I was informed of the bare-handed destruction of the demon Elder. Luckily, this company of fine warriors and I entered the scene when this beast appeared. I am no friend to demons and I received great satisfaction felling this one like wild game. Wild game, however, gets my respect when I hunt for it." The warriors laughed at this, nodding their heads simultaneously.

"I could not destroy a demon by myself, for I did not know how without a large herd. I met Minos on my way from the Second Circle, and he bade me stay and visit. The King Judge showed me the spell. He demonstrated on an imp, which also, interestingly, became a cloud of smoke at its demise. I was not certain the spell would work on a demon, especially one so powerful, but once I saw the look of terror on its face, my doubts departed. Also, I am weary, as Minos said I would be from casting the spell. So you see there are far too many signs to ignore." Chiron looked at Militus.

"Militus, you were one of my finest students. I am proud to see you have won the admiration of these able warriors." Chiron surveyed the proud men, who were smiling and staring at this centaur anomaly. Chiron was spoken of many times by Militus as the inspiration for the strategies used in many of their mock battles. Now they were really face to face with the centaur, and the stature and strength of the Halfling were far more awesome than any tale.

They all stayed in each other's company, not unwary of the danger around them, for hours, speaking to the centaur, asking questions about his life and adventures. Chiron regaled them with stories of his students, the harpies in the circle below, and his study of medicines and healing herbs. Aristotle, who had been a go-between of the humans and centaurs, had shared much of this information in his logs, but many of the warriors were not so inclined to read. In return for the stories of his adventures, the men shared the fruits of Limbo, which Chiron ate readily. He had earlier filled up at the pool of the First Waters, cleansing himself soon after. He would have stayed in the pool far longer were he less responsible; he had not bathed since his entry into Hell, and the waters rejuvenating effects were quite addictive.

Darius and Mortuus almost forgot that they were going to be leaving Limbo. It was Militus who finally snapped them back into the current reality.

"I am sorry my friends – you will have to go with Chiron." Militus looked slightly worried. "I did not want to send you out, but there are events and challenges ahead of us that we must prepare for. We have overcome two demons; we must not press our good fortune by remaining in place. Better to wander safely outside the walls than to be captured. Master Chiron, my old teacher, you must go soon."

The fugitive pair, Darius and Mortuus, returned to a gloomy state, but neither could help but feel better about the fact that they would be among the great centaur for their trek to the Seventh Circle.

The warriors departed sadly. Militus dispersed them back toward Bremen, where they were to join Benjamin at the Hall of Science. Chiron, just before the warriors began their return trip, thanked them for their hospitality and their courage, and declared all 'Centaur Friends and Allies', a gesture of honor on his part, as they cheered and thanked him repeatedly. In return, they vowed to respect the centaur race, and to honor them as friends and allies, and of course welcomed guests to

Limbo should the opportunity arise. The warriors bowed as the Master

centaur placed his hand on his chest and nodded, then turned to leave.

Militus walked with the group, unsure of what might come out of

the sky. They were between Graz and Almere, and the original

traveling party of Barak, Mortuus, Darius, Socius and Clavius had

passed the mines many hours ago on the return toward Bremen in an

effort to find Militus and Benjamin when the demon attacked them.

Chiron kept his eyes upward, his crossbow ready to launch deadly

projectiles instantly. His strength was slowly returning after eating the

strange fruits; he hoped to be fully restored before exiting Limbo.

Barak and Clavius were deep in thought, sad and happy at the same

time. They had a revelation before that they wanted to speak of,

especially to Militus and Socius, but they would not talk in front of

Chiron, Darius or Mortuus, because, known only to them, the actions of

the three had to be natural, not forced by any knowledge of prophecies.

Soon, they reached the path outside of the pit. Militus and Barak

walked ahead until they could see the path was clear of demons. Barak

ran ahead, down the circling path to the inside of the excavated hole,

yelling for Eruo, Abreo or Exaro to come out of the mine. He wanted to

be sure that none of the smithy demons were inside picking up processed ore. Militus waited on the upper ledge, the rest of the group hid themselves behind the rock piles in the front of the path.

Militus observed the pit center, and after a long while, Barak came out of the mine, three dust covered miners trailing behind him. Militus could not hear, but he was aware that Barak was speaking to the miners through his body language and gestures. Finally, Barak and the three miners looked at the upper ledge toward Militus, and Barak waved his arms to signal the party to come down to the mine entrance. Militus took a last look around, and then whistled in a high pitch. Chiron, Socius, Clavius, Mortuus and Darius walked out onto the ledge. Now the three soiled miners only stared in shocked surprise and awe. Abreo grinned a toothy grin, the whites of his teeth contrasting brightly with his dirty face. Exaro and another miner, Eruos, a taller thin framed man watched stood frozen in disbelief. What happened next they could not have prepared for.

A demon appeared, high up against the misty ceiling; it was flying from the same direction as the smithy demons, but it was not like the smithy demon they had seen enter the pit on their first visit. This one was much more similar to the demon they had recently destroyed, more human in countenance. The creature spotted them and descended quickly, almost dropping to the ground.

Chiron was the first on the offensive. Before the rest of the group knew it, the human-like beast had crashed to the ground at their feet, surprised and flailing in agony, outraged at the impudence of being attacked. Chiron had managed to put six arrows in key locations to disable the creature, and all before it hit the path in front of them, such was his skill. It had not expected rebuttal – no creature in Hell ever fought back, nor would it have mattered if they did. These were the strongest, free roaming denizens in Hell, second only to the Fallen. Now it was writhing on its' back, inhuman screeches emanating so loud and piercing that Darius thought he would pass out from the pain in his ears. Between shrieks, Militus yelled out to Chiron.

"Now Chiron, before it casts any spells!" yelled Militus. Chiron spoke his spell, and the creature stopped and stared in horror as it began a slow dissolve into dark smoke, leaving only a final stabbing scream. Stunned at the quick destruction of the demon, Barak and company sat on the ground to recover from the encounter. It had exhausted him just by stress and fear. The three miners walked up toward the group,

smiling and excited by what they had just witnessed. Barak was the
first to comment.

"Well. That was easy enou-"

It was he who saw the next shadow and yelled, but too late.
Another demon had appeared overhead when they were all looking
downward at the smoke of the demised beast. Mortuus was hit first,
clawed in his face and sent flying via kick into a wall of rock. The
demon hit them each of the traveling party and the three miners, fast
and hard, and sent each airborne over a ledge or into a wall of stone. It
was enraged by their destruction of the other demon, and it slashed its
claws at Chiron the most, ripping out pieces of his rear and side rib
flank. The centaur was bleeding heavily, and a still reeling Militus
jumped up and grabbed it from behind, pulling his arm around its neck.
This was a futile move, he knew, but he would think of nothing else in
the moment to relieve his old master, if for only temporarily. To his
surprise and slight relief, Darius joined him, grabbing the left arm of
the demon, as it suddenly opened its wings against both men violently.
They were thrown easily, and the creature turned and targeted the pair
of badly wounded men.

Walking toward Militus, it ripped a claw through the air so fast that Militus could hear his neck snap. He crumpled to the ground, as the demon turned toward Darius. Barak had gotten to his feet, and, picking up an arrow moved behind the demon, preparing to stab it in the back. The demon, effortlessly spread its left wing out without flinching the rest of its body, and Barak flew 20 meters into a wall. A spate of blood marked where he struck the wall. Darius lay on the path, wounded and terrified, awaiting the gory violence.

"Bascaria – batah!" A voice, but not Chiron's', came over the shoulder of the demon. Mortuus had cast the spell. The demon stopped, and knew fear, its face became gnarled and warped, and with a loud screech the beast darkened and floated off into the heights, dispersing with the movement of the air. The joy and relief of the group was more overwhelming, but they were all seriously injured. Chiron laid down on his side and was bleeding profusely, pulling his skin together where the demon had ripped it open. Mortuus was limping weakly as he tried to stand up, looking around at his fellow travelers. He managed to walk, but then hobbled over to where Militus lay, his head bent in an unnatural position because of his broken neck. Mortuus instinctively placed his hands on the base of Militus' skull, and muttered a few

115

words. Militus' neck began to straighten, and his head turned back to its correct position. Militus, feeling suddenly well again, sat up. Mortuus had healed his wound by magical incantation; Militus, because of the extreme pain he was in, could not hear anything more than mumbling emanate from Mortuus. Mortuus, in a weakened state, lay flat on the ground to rest. Darius, severely bruised, went to help up the three miners, each of whom had been knocked into a wall. Socius, Barak and Clavius were down on the next level of the path - they had been thrown over the edge by the force of the blows.

"Son of a harpy!" said a sore and embittered Eruos.

"I will concur, Eruos. Socius! Are you well?" Abreo stood up on his own before Darius could reach him, looking over the edge at Barak, Clavius and Socius; they were getting up, helping each other to stand. "Darius, see to Exaro, he looks awful! Oh wait. That is how he always looks; never mind." The group laughed, even in their great pain. Exaro half-scowled, half-smiled.

"You are very humorous. For an idiot."

They were shaken up by the incident, and for many hours they stayed to regenerate, and each kept his eyes peeled toward the ceiling of mist over Limbo. Militus went to retrieve his soldiers, and returned much later with a dozen men, plus glass pitchers of the healing waters, fruits and herbs. They all drank deeply, the most damaged being urged on by the warriors who had brought the pitchers. Militus sent six men to watch for demons on both sides of the pit, and he presented Mortuus with a broadsword that befitted his large size. On the heels of this, another warrior gave a spare short sword to Darius. The pair of fugitives were gracious and thanked their benefactors. Finally, Chiron spoke.

"Angel...Mortuus – that is your real name?" asked Chiron. "It seems unusual. I know of the angelic realms and Mortuus does not seem to be a name from the angelic tongue."

"That name was provided by Aristotle upon his awakening, it means 'dead.' Do not worry; it is not his real name. That we do not know. " stated Socius.

"Interesting. I have many questions for you Angel Mortuus," said Chiron. "I generally distrust Fallen, but I sense you are... different."

Mortuus had felt some mistrust from Chiron since meeting him. It saddened him, but he understood, especially considering where they were.

"You do not trust me, Lord Chiron." The centaur gazed silently at Mortuus.

"I am unsure. The Fallen I have ever interacted with would hardly bother with me and my kind. But your own, the Fallen, have placed you and many others in a comatose state, a prison of eternal sleep. I do not know why, though I will assume you are their enemy. My fear is that you will suddenly recall who you are, unfriendly to centaur-folk." This struck a chord in Mortuus. His fear was to awaken his memories and consider his friends as enemies. It was a worry that he suppressed, but would not speak of. The idea was, at this point in his awakening, a monster he would not be able to overcome.

"Fair enough," replied Mortuus. "Truthfully, I have harbored this concern since discovering part of my identity. I would say I do not have any recollection of a past and I see no reason to have any problems with you or your fellow centaurs. Should my memories heal, I will honor–"

"Do not make promises you may not be able to keep. I hold you to nothing; I only wish to free a friend from the Fallen overlords. There are no oaths you need swear to."

"Very well," returned Mortuus. He felt no more need to speak to Chiron on this subject. Chiron seemed a creature that would not judge Mortuus by his words. There was a moment of uncomfortable silence before Militus queried Mortuus.

"Mortuus, how did you feel after casting that spell?" he asked. Mortuus concerns were pushed aside. Militus was uncomfortable before, but could do nothing to alter the conversation between angel and centaur, nor did he feel it was his place to.

"I felt weakened, yet more powerful at the same time, as if I had stirred pleasant memories, if you can understand that. It is an awkward explanation, but I seemed to lose energy, causing me the weakness. At the same time, movement of the energy seems to have made me feel…better, as if flowing and more alive. Why do you ask, Militus?"

"I needed to see that your experience was different from others, like Clavius. Master Chiron, how did you feel?" asked the seasoned warrior to the centaur.

"I was quite weakened, almost sickened with fatigue." Militus nodded to himself, his theory confirmed.

"Ahh. You see, Mortuus. Being of the angel folk, it is important for you to flow magically, to use your magic, practice it, and explore it.

When the energy is not used, it becomes as stagnant as still water. Clavius, you recall how you felt when you tried some of the angelic magic?"

"Yes – I could hardly move for some time if I tried any sort of spell – I listened to the demons cast the spells to excavate the mine in its earlier days, and when I experimented and tried the spells elsewhere in Limbo, it was as if I had performed all the work of the spell myself. I attempted to move a boulder, and when I cast the spell, I fell to the ground and could not stand up again for a long while. Illumination spells tired me much less."

"Interesting," added Socius. "I would like to try some of these spells sometime to see-"

"You must wait until we get Aristotle back here, Socius!" Militus was stern. Socius fumed for a moment, and then consigned this to the protectiveness of the teachers and warriors who raised him. Militus sighed deeply. "I only wish to protect you, Socius. I apologize for my rashness."

"It is time we depart Limbo for the seventh circle. Mortuus, Darius and I will leave all of you from here. Eruos, will you guide us now?"

asked Chiron. Eruos spoke and the bitterness he had expressed earlier had disappeared.

"Follow me, my friends," He addressed the angel, centaur and Darius, "I do not know when we will meet again – if you return us our fellow Aristotle, we will be in your debt." Socius seconded the notion. Eruos arose, Mortuus bowed goodbye to all the warriors, to Socius, Militus, Clavius and Barak. Darius followed suit. Mortuus spoke one more time.

"I am in your debt my friends. If I never get back here I will at least have been here and always have these memories, if none other." He looked at Socius. "We will rescue our friend Aristotle from these beasts, Socius. You saved me, assisted me greatly by daring to venture outside the gate, when you could have remained safely behind and not placed yourself in opposition of the corrupt Elders. I will not forget your kindness."

"As will I," said Darius. Clenched up with the fear of leaving Limbo, he had to push himself to speak. The words choked out of his throat. Outer hell caused great pain just in its anticipation. But he had hope this time, something not available outside, because he could return. A light in the darkness that was outer Hell. Just then a distant, shrill whistle sounded. Militus motioned his men to watch the air above

the pit. The warriors focused their gaze upward, an equal number of

men watching from each direction.

"Good luck my friends – you must go now. The men have seen

something, and I think you had better disappear into the mine. Hurry!"

Militus shouted as he looked back and forth between the three and the

soldiers above. Into the opening and down the darkened cave they ran,

following Eruos. Exaro and Abreo trailed the three.

Once they were far enough into the cave, Eruos pulled a switch on

the wall and the entrance they had entered closed up with a snap. It was

as if the wall behind them never had an opening at all. The journey

through the mine was a test of its own for both centaur and angel.

Neither creature was well-disposed to the close overhangs and tight

openings that composed the mine. The miners asked questions of both

Mortuus and Chiron, and their queries were useful distractions from the

almost overwhelming claustrophobia. Chiron had trouble fitting inside

more than a few openings, though for the most part he could squeeze

into the caverns and miniature passages. The three had no idea how

long or far their journey would be to the exit. Mortuus was of an aviary

race of beings, and began to slowly feel the walls and ceilings enclosing him; this was different than Clavius' underground, particularly the lighting and dimensions of space. He recalled the fear and unknowing in the aftermath of his awakening, and how he had finally stumbled to the surface exit from the underground of the Seventh Circle. Though he was far different now, memories of that unpleasantness and panic were welling up inside him, as if he was in a dungeon.

Angels did not belong in the dungeons of Hell.

Chapter 54

Back to Circle Seven

It had been a long, hazardous journey to get back to Chiron's place and people. The three had left the secret exit from the mine into the putrid sleet fall of the Third Circle, completely bypassing the Second Circle. Eruos had not disclosed where he would lead them, though he had several exits on the Second Circle, and was even working on a passage to the Fourth currently. The trip through the mine was grueling for Mortuus, and humiliating for Chiron, who had to be pushed through many openings by his rear end because of his size. Darius had no qualms except for the dirtiness of their surroundings, having enjoyed being cleansed in Limbo after many centuries.

The three emerged with great sighs of relief, though short lived, as they faced outer Hell's sound and stink. Looking around as they walked onto the landscape, Chiron saw the three-headed giant dog Cerberus not far away, being harassed by a pack of eighteen imps. The beasts were throwing rocks at the giant dog as he backed away whimpering against the wall, a short distance from where they had just emerged.

"I had assumed this monstrous dog was far fiercer than these imps, Chiron," whispered Mortuus. "Why does it cringe away from them when it could easily rip them apart?"

"The dog is probably trained to obey Fallen and their workers," guessed Chiron, "Imagine the cruelty they must have inflicted upon it to gain its obeisance if they would cut off the wings of their own."

Motioning Mortuus and Darius to be silent, Chiron walked silently in the opposite direction, tiptoeing as well as a large half-human, half-horse could. They were nearly out of sight when Mortuus accidentally stepped onto the frozen face of a human buried in the slushy vomit.

"Damn animal! Watch where you step, filthy dog! Isn't it bad enough you chew our entrails…" the imprisoned man's face blinked his slushed-over eyes, looking at Mortuus more clearly, and then started yelling. "Fugitives! How dare you tread on me!" yelled the voice of the bloated face, as Mortuus jumped back in shock. "Fugitives! Fugitives!" repeated the man, yelling at the top of his lungs. Chiron looked back toward where the large dog had been cornered by the imps, trying to see, hoping they were out of earshot. The sight of the pack running and flying in their direction, confirmed they were not. Mortuus, now angry and irritated, kicked the shouting distended face, and the man quieted immediately as he spit blood and teeth.

Darius, who was in the rear of the three, pulled the short sword the warrior had given him earlier. It was heavy for its size, but Darius could see that it would easily cut whatever it touched, so finely honed was the sharpened blade. Mortuus pulled the sword given him by Militus, and he and Chiron walked alongside of Darius as the pack drew near. Darius, although emboldened to fight alongside his companions, had never yet fought one of the smallish vermin; his face was the picture of fear.

"Stand apart!" commanded Chiron, "They will divide and we will each have fewer to kill. Darius – this is your first time to defend against these creatures; do not underestimate them, but no matter your fear or pain, you must continue to fight."

Mortuus turned toward Darius.

"Be brave my friend. Let your rage power the fight." The imps were nearer, and Chiron dispatched several at a distance before they were on the group. Two flyers went down, and another six of the demon miniatures smoked instantly. This encouraged all three, but the pack was still large enough to be of concern.

Darius, shaken, barely managed his sword, and, ignoring the warnings of Barak earlier, spoke the spell he had heard both Mortuus and Chiron utter in Limbo at the pack, causing three of the creatures to morph into dark clouds. Casting the spell enraged the imps so much that they fought harder and with more daring and ferocity than Mortuus and Chiron had ever seen, and Darius was severely disabled for using it. He fell to the ground in a hunched-over clump, weakened so much that he was unable to move or lend assist any further.

Chiron, irritated, assessed the matter with incredible speed, and quickly hefted the immobilized Darius onto his back as he spun and loosed his bow into the swarm. Popping sounds emitted from the creatures, and sometimes twice at a time as the centaurs' great archery skills answered the growls of the imps.

Some of the creatures had gotten to the fighting pair. One imp, a flyer, landed on the back of Chiron, and had begun to rip at the slumped form of Darius, who could barely make a sound in his physically immobilized state. Another pair of imps had gotten a hold of Chiron's rear legs, biting into his powerful haunches, causing him great pain, and distraction. The centaur staggered for a moment before shaking them off and firing into them in a fury. They had done some

127

damage, as he would not walk well until Darius had recovered a long time later.

Mortuus, however, had suffered the most bloodying from the attack. His back had been ripped open, and his clean, new robes shredded and bloodied. Mortuus sight was blocked by the smoke of the recently dispatched imps, allowing the remaining imps to slip through the smokescreen and get at Mortuus before he could see them coming. He was swinging wildly in his pain and panic, and accidentally sliced into his own leg trying to get free. When it was finally done, and all the imps had been destroyed, the three spent many hours regenerating, and Chiron retrieved his arrows. They had no alternative, even though the putrid vomit laden sleet was overwhelming their senses. Cerberus did not find them, and they thought he must be avoiding the pack, unaware they had been exterminated.

"I have not seen so many of these beasts in one place since my awakening. Do you suppose they-" said Mortuus. He was cut off by Chiron's reply.

"-were looking for you? Yes, I believe so." replied Chiron. "We must move before anymore arrive. The demons believe you to be hiding out in Limbo, and so they are focusing their energies there."

"Why did they attack the dog?" asked Mortuus.

"They are undisciplined – without their masters to order their actions, they slip away to mischief and cruelty, even when it is forbidden or illogical. In my circle, we dispatched many of these who wandered near enough before they were able to determine it was a danger zone for their kind."

"Foolish beasts, then," said Mortuus. "How is Darius doing?"

"He will have to be carried on my back for some time," said Chiron. "I would have you know that this is humiliating for my kind; to be a beast of burden is a high insult. *I* am not belittled by helping your friend, but my kind would find this disparaging, and some might challenge my leadership. When we approach my circle, I will instruct you on what to expect and how to act."

"Do you wish me to carry Darius, Lord Chiron? I would rather you had your hands free; you are the best fighter among us." Chiron looked at Mortuus.

"I can carry him easily – I only wished to inform you of the nuances of my culture. Thank you for the offer."

Finally, after a long trek through the vomit precipitation, the three found the path that lead down to the Fourth Circle. They had a quick run in with Plutus. Chiron did not hesitate. He filled Plutus' hide with enough arrows to slow him down until they could get to the Fifth Circle. Mortuus and Chiron had anticipated Plutus. They had not, however, anticipated the two fugitive hunter demons that appeared in the distance. They were found.

Chiron had discussed a strategy for dealing with demons with Mortuus as they were climbing down through the mine. The spell was to be used when they encountered only one demon; two demons would have to be disabled, filled with Chiron's' arrows, then strangled by Mortuus and Chiron to conserve Mortuus' magical energy. It was during this exchange in the mine between the angel and the centaur that Darius got his notion to use the angel magic. He would not do so again this trip.

Chiron pulled his bow back as the pair approached. They were cursing the centaur in their half-growl, half-human tones, and it reminded him of his life among the humans that hunted and exterminated him and his kind.

One particular hunting party had attempted to corner Chiron against the side of a sheer mountain wall, cliffs high above; they were outcasts from their village, criminals, misfits, untouchables who earned their lowly status by their own actions. Chiron knew this because he had friends in the village with whom he would secretly meet. When the three village criminals were exiled, they grouped together and decided that bringing back the head of the Master Centaur, Chiron himself, would earn them the right to live among their fellow humans in the village. Chiron waited, knowing their plans to stalk him, and drew them into a large brushy area, a naturally formed maze. When they re-emerged later, far from where they entered, Chiron waited, and had his bow drawn. They were cursing him in the same low, guttural sounds as he now heard emanating from the demons.

When one of the men attempted to throw his spear at Chiron, Chiron dispatched him quickly, redrawing his bow before the others knew what had happened. When they became aware, they ran from the centaur in a panic, into the cave of a napping mother bear and her young cubs. Chiron sealed the cave until the screams had faded away.

The rage from that time in Chiron's life washed over him, and he used it to fuel a speedy delivery of high speed arrows into the two demons. They screamed and shrieked in pain and rage for a few seconds. The barrage of arrows stuck into their throats and silenced them. It was a relief to dispatch the disabled pair. Chiron kneeled onto the throat of one of the demons with his front leg (the demon was very strong Chiron thought, even full of arrows). After a few seconds, the demon transformed into smoke. Mortuus wrapped his arm around the throat of the other, and it, too, became a floating smoke shape.

In the Fifth circle, along the bank, Phlegyas had been standing by the shore next to his skiff. Chiron addressed his friend, and Phlegyas stared at him blankly. The centaur stopped his movement, and Darius and Mortuus followed, sensing the danger. Looking around quickly, Chiron and Mortuus could see no imminent danger. Chiron looked into the face of his friend. Phlegyas was different looking from their first meeting. Mortuus looked, closely, and then yelled his warning.

"DEMON!" His angel sight caught the creature in its disguised form. Reacting violently, the creature that was almost Phlegyas quickly morphed, grabbing onto Mortuus. This creature was so strong that Mortuus could hardly move within its grip. It spoke, a harsh, fast word, Mortuus remembered the word, then felt the strength draining as his limbs froze in place. Mortuus was paralyzed, just as he had been in Limbo.

Chiron saw Mortuus' situation. He approached the transforming demon, thrusting his small sword through its neck. Chiron repeated the paralysis spell - he had just heard it - and watched the beast freeze, then slide off of his sword onto the squishy ground with a splash. Chiron sank to the ground next to the beast; unable to move, so complete was his exhaustion. Darius, the only one of the three able to stand, though barely, placed his knee on the throat of the paralyzed demon, leaning into it and slicing it weakly across the chest and abdomen until the creature finally smoked. Chiron struggled to regain his footing and gave Darius a weak smile of approval, then collapsed again to the wet ground. They remained there for a short time.

Chiron arose first, shakily. Mortuus finally felt his strength return as his movement was no longer hindered. They removed much of the putrid slush that had been on them since the Third Circle by rolling around on the waterlogged ground. It was full of roots and small vegetation, which seemed to be what held it together. Thankfully, they did not have to enter the river to wash off.

They found Phlegyas in a weakened state on the flaming tower side of the Styx, at the landing where Mortuus and Chiron had first boarded. He had been stunned by the demon, which ravaged the oarsman grotesquely with his claws after disabling him, then used a spell to transform into the likeness of Phlegyas. Phlegyas, a bloody mess, required a long regeneration period. The group stayed with him, though they wished to hurry through the gates, into Dis and toward the relative safety of Chiron's circle. It was this charity that saved them from capture. After a long time, Phlegyas was able to speak to them, weakly at first.

"My friends, you must not enter the gates. The Fallen know of the angel's escape." Phlegyas motioned toward Mortuus. "You are able to defeat one or two at once? Behind the gates you will find more, many more, searching between the tombs; they remain near this very gate. You must not pass this way."

"We wish to get to my circle, Phlegyas. How will we pass through the tombs?" asked Chiron. "There is no other way to -"

"There is, Chiron. I will take you when I am regenerated." Phlegyas paused, "Why does the angel follow you, Chiron? Was not Limbo more ideal?" He laughed with this question – it was not really a question.

"The beasts have entered Limbo – in fact, they have been there all along, Phlegyas. One of them was disguised as an Elder! They have infiltrated even the 'virtuous' humans. We left in haste, as they were nearing us. Two we destroyed just prior to our exit." Phlegyas looked

surprised, and contemplated this news.

"Hell is changing. And you, angel, what will you do? They will

return you to the dark dungeon under the tombs. Many demons pursue

you." Phlegyas was grim. He started to move around, then, picked

himself up. They got into his boat and left the mucky landing, but

instead of turning to the left toward the opposite signal tower, they

went right, heading into the deep mist of the Styx. It was a long, slow

trip, and on many occasions, the humans were looking out of the water,

staring at the strange, immense frame of Chiron. Some were too near

the boat, and Phlegyas cracked their skulls with a deftness of oar

swinging skill. After Phlegyas swung, the river dwellers scattered,

returning to their madness, gnashing, tearing and ripping their fellows

long after the skiff was out of sight.

Phlegyas was taking the three to another entrance to Dis, and

explained the alternate passageway that had been built into the far side

of Dis' protective wall. The small doorway had been part of a much

larger opening, long closed by the Fallen. Originally, Dis had two large

gates. The second gate was rarely used, and so very few, besides

wandering imps and demons, along with a handful of fugitives, had ever encountered the opening. Somehow, the landing in front of the gate had eroded over time and simply disappeared into the Styx. The Fallen sent their worker demons to seal the gate, along with the appropriate spells. The demons, ever mistrusting, left a small doorway that could only be opened with magic. They had used a combination spell that was difficult to cast.

Phlegyas had learned the combination spell from a demon. The demon had recited the spell right front of Phlegyas. At the time, Phlegyas could not understand the spell, but he was able to figure out how to use it eventually. The only problem was that it was a one way spell; no one could return back through once they had entered into Dis.

This was not normally a consideration. No problem, unless you were the ferryman of the Styx and left your skiff behind the door. The three chuckled at the oarsman's wry humor. Phlegyas had to blow his horn to bring the Fallen once he discovered the unidirectional property of the doorway. It was easy to get out of, however; he informed them he had been jumped by some rogue demons, and had his skiff taken. The Fallen brought back his skiff angrily, but Phlegyas knew they had no choice but to believe him – the demons were often unstable and lied easily.

The skiff arrived at the small opening without incident; aside from the inhabitants of the swamp nearing the skiff to see Chiron and a few skull-cracking swats of the oar from Phlegyas, no other occurrences inhibited their boat ride. Phlegyas, having rarely had company, spoke of his own life and exploits, telling the tales that led up to his death at the hands of Apollo. Mortuus and Darius listened intently, enjoying the stories, except, of course, for the death of Phlegyas' daughter. The pain of this event showed even on the grim countenance of Chiron.

Phlegyas, in life, was King of the Lapiths. He had two children; one, a daughter, was named Coronis. The God Apollo had taken a deep liking to Coronis, and even had blessed Phlegyas with a prosperous kingdom. Phlegyas, knowing of his daughters' fickleness with male suitors, had warned Coronis not to partner with Apollo. Phlegyas paid his homage to Apollo regularly, and honorably, as did all the subjects of his nation, and even named Apollo the father of their country. But Coronis, unable to withstand the pressing of Apollo for her love, fell into a relationship, and each evening would meet with the god in the forest near the palace. On certain evenings, Apollo would not appear, busy with some of the many works of gods, unknown to Coronis. In her youthfulness, and insecurity, she was wooed away during one of these nights, by a handsome young man, Ischys, who had been watching her meetings with Apollo. After a few nights seeing Coronis alone and sad, Ischys approached.

Phlegyas knew of his daughters' interactions with Apollo, and had men follow and watch the princess. He had charged them with keeping any and all would-be suitors away. On many occasions there had been royal suitors who visited and requested consideration for the hand of Coronis. Some, of great wealth and fame, could not understand the refusal of Phlegyas. They pursued the princess, and met with mysterious, accidental deaths.

Phlegyas could not stand to lose his daughter, and would have sacrificed a hundred suitors for her life if he had to. The men who watched Coronis were unaware of the forest visits by Apollo; when it was time for their meeting, the entire palace, everyone who worked inside and out, were put to sleep to provide Coronis an undisturbed walk to her rendezvous. This became automatic, occurring each night whether Apollo appeared or not.

Soon, Coronis became pregnant, and Apollo had a crow follow her to assure her safety during the pregnancy. It was on one of the nights that Coronis had met with her other lover, Ischys that the crow returned to Apollo with his report. The god, outraged, had his sister, the goddess

Artemis, kill Coronis shortly after giving birth. The child was taken by

Apollo. Phlegyas swiftly had Ischys murdered, and soon went to the

temple of Apollo at Delphi, and burnt it to the ground. Apollo struck

Phlegyas down in person, and he awoke before the Fallen. The Fallen

charged the king with boating the Styx.

It was a long while before anyone spoke. Mortuus could see the

pain of these times on the face of Phlegyas.

"Phlegyas, did you ever find out what happened to the child of

Coronis and Apollo?" asked Chiron.

"No." answered Phlegyas. "I was dead soon after Apollo carried

off the babe; I barely saw my grandson. I saw only the back of Artemis

as she vanished from my daughter's bedside. Why do you ask?"

"I am sorry, Phlegyas. So much has happened since I left my

circle; I neglected to consider you would not be aware." Phlegyas face

showed a grave concern at hearing this news of Chiron. What was he

sorry for? Had something happened to his grandson as well as his

daughter? "Apollo gave the child to *me* to raise. Your grandson's name

was Asclepius. I instructed him in medicines and hunting, and in his

day, he was as famous for medicines as Hercules was for strength."

Phlegyas eyes widened in surprise and delight. "Asclepius specialized in the medicines and incantations that have been used for love and sickness. His skill was legendary." Phlegyas smiled broadly. He had heard of Chiron and the plight of the centaur race, and had wished to intervene on their behalf. His counselors and court nobles advised against it. To their dismay, Phlegyas proclaimed that no citizen of his Kingdom should ever harm the Master Centaur, and later expanded his edict to include all centaur kind. This turned out to be a difficult law to enforce, due to the mounting hatred and violent actions of a small minority of his subjects, and the drunken misbehavior of a small minority of centaurs. Chiron and the centaurs did not disappear until long after Phlegyas had been murdered by Apollo.

"Then I am grateful to you, and in your debt for all time my friend." Phlegyas was exuberant. "Tell me, I have only one fear, is my grandson in Limbo, or any other place of Hell?"

"Not as far as I have knowledge of. Aristotle has not been able to penetrate to the farthest depths, but I have heard no news of Asclepius' since my arrival." Chiron, normally grim in speaking manner, stared at Phlegyas, and for a moment, smiled. The Ferryman who was once King lost all control of his grin.

"Thank you, my friend. Thank you."

Chapter 55

Guests on the Blood River

Pholus could not believe his eyes. Sitting near the rocky slope of the Seventh Circle with several of the centaur commanders, he stared as Chiron emerged from the mist. Following behind the leader centaur were two humans, one large and one small and gaunt, and more astonishingly, one whom Pholus had chased away on many occasions, the Minotaur. The group of four was walking down the slope in single file fashion, and Pholus knew this was at the behest of his friend Chiron. Pholus and the commanders, Tacitus among them, stood frozen in place, mouths agape at this very odd entourage. Chiron, seeing Pholus and his commanders at the base of the slope, changed course and headed in the direction of the meeting of the centaur leadership.

Ironically, Pholus had called this meeting after Chiron had not returned for more than forty turns. The Second in Command of the centaur herds had Titan trot the entire circumference of the Seventh Circle and report each time he completed a lap. Pholus began to worry when Chiron did not reappear after the twenty-fifth round, but withheld taking action for another fifteen rounds, considering he really had no idea how long Chiron would be away. The herds had begun to whisper, rumors of their missing master circulated widely, and Pholus gathered his leaders to initiate counter-measures. The commanders, only a small sampling of the total number of herd leaders, were those whom Pholus trusted the most. They did not include Nessus in their number.

When Chiron and his strange herd approached, Pholus and the commanders followed the usual protocol, though none took their eyes off of the Minotaur. Even the thinner, frail human seemed wary of the bull-like beast, looking behind him with each step. The Minotaur did not miss the fearful wariness of the human; every so often he would emit a low rumbling growl, stopping only when the group neared the meeting centaur commanders. Chiron returned their bows and introduced his queer company, though not without prefacing with an explanation of his arrival.

"Commanders, I am happy to see you all. I have returned from a lengthy and not uneventful journey, and I have much news to report. I know all here to be loyal and faithful to our centaur kind, and the wisest and most trusted leaders of the herds. I know this from my own observations, and those of Commander Pholus, who has summoned you in a most timely manner, unbeknownst even to himself. I have returned from a visit to the First Circle, the area known as Limbo, and with those I would have you accept on my word as friends to centaur kind." At this, the leaders scanned the guests of Chiron, feeling at ease to do so now that he had requested their acceptance, and they scrutinized even the Minotaur, who stared back at each commander in turn.

Chiron continued, "This is a most unusual request, Commanders. I understand, and I will assure you I have not lost my senses. I ask your discretion - do not speak with any outside of this group of what I tell you here and now. Do you agree to this?" The commanders bowed deeply, indicating their oath of silence as Chiron moved to the bull-man. "I give you Asterion, a Halfling, like ourselves, though he is a bull Halfling, and his halves are reversed from ours. He has been wandering the rocky slope, his assigned patrol by the Fallen masters. Like us, he was brutalized for his differences by the humans, and in turn defied them by being the monster they had labeled him."

Chiron moved to Darius. "This is Darius, former slave, sentenced to the Vestibule. Yes, he is a fugitive. He and two others escaped their aimless running. His fellows were captured by flying demons, and taken to the Eighth Circle early after their escape."

Chiron moved toward Mortuus. "And here, though you may find it hard to believe, is the strangest guest to our circle. You may have thought that would be Asterion, and you would be wrong. Tell me, Tacitus, what do you see here?" Chiron motioned toward Mortuus.

"I see a human, a large human, but only human."

"Pholus. Tell me what you see," requested Chiron. Pholus had a puzzled expression on his face.

"Human." The remaining commander's nodded agreement as Chiron polled the group one by one.

"As I thought," said Chiron. Mortuus prepared himself for their reactions, and that of Asterion, who also did not know.

"This is Mortuus. He is our friend. And he is of the Fallen."

Chapter 56

New Tricks for Old Centaurs

The commanders, including Pholus sat there stunned at the revelation Chiron had just given them. Friend? Fallen? This could not be - the Fallen were the jailers, the cruel prison wardens of Hell for thousands of years. The air was silent, but the expressions on the faces of the herd leaders spoke volumes. Chiron broke the silence after a long pause.

"You have said nothing, Commanders. Do you not have questions? I believe you see why there is a necessity for prudence." One of the commanders spoke.

"Master Chiron, truly, I wonder how this came to be, and I would ask that you share the story of your journey to the First Circle, that we may gather the pieces of this puzzle together and enjoy your travel tale. It has been too long since we have been imprisoned on this boiling river of Hell, and I would hear of the outside, even though it be Hell."

Chiron smiled, relieved, and the other commanders grunted and neighed their agreement, and joy to hear a new story, a fresh adventure.

146

After thousands of years, it would be like a jug of cold water in a desert. Mortuus, also relieved, sat down on the gravelly ground, and Darius joined him. Mortuus had felt the scrutiny of Chiron change as they fought their way to the Seventh Circle together, and the introduction to the Commander centaurs confirmed this. Only Asterion seemed to be upset, but no one noticed. A low rumble again emanated from deep within the Halfling, who was glaring at the angel and causing alarm with the Commanders and Chiron.

"Asterion, please. You must trust what I tell you. He is our friend," said Chiron. Asterion continued to glare, but ceased his growling.

"I will trust your judgment, friend Chiron. But I will watch the Fallen one carefully." With that, Asterion sat on the ground, looking at Mortuus periodically, distrustfully, and causing the angel discomfort.

Chiron told his story, about his ascent up the rocky slope, and his meeting with Asterion. His encounter with Plutus, the once demigod transformed into wolf demon by the Fallen, his meeting with Minos (and Asterion, for the first time since his early youth, wept at this); finding Charon missing (and he would defer to Mortuus and Darius to fill in details of this later), plus the events of Limbo, including the demons who had been dissipated into smoke. The centaurs recalled the

147

events of long ago when they had shot the demon left behind by the Fallen and thrown it into the river. Chiron finished with his entry through the back entrance of the Sixth Circle and meeting Asterion, who had been evading the demons as they searched for Mortuus near the front gate of Dis. The Master Centaur then asked Mortuus to explain his origin as he had on the trek through the mines of Limbo, from his trip to the Vestibule to his entry to Limbo. The commanders were in awe as Darius interrupted and told of Mortuus' defeat of the demon Elder barehanded. In all, this was the best round of storytelling the centaurs could remember, all the better for the destruction of their common enemy, the demon workers.

"Commanders," said Chiron, "I am happy to have shared these events with you, and I would speak with you of matter more pressing to myself and our human and angel friends. There is a human recently captured and removed to the forbidden area."

"Your friend. The teacher, Aristotle," said one of the commanders. Chiron looked at him squarely, confused as to how he knew of Aristotle. Chiron had considered his meetings with Aristotle to be discrete, kept from his fellows for his and their sakes. Humans were not liked by centaurs, and Aristotle would be safer if the herds did not

know of him, in case of an uprising or challenge.

"Why…yes. How do you know of my meetings with Aristotle?"

"We have heard of it, mostly from Commander Nessus, Master

Chiron, though we thought he told us only to sow discord in his usual

manner, and so we kept it to ourselves and forbade him to speak of it

with the herds lest we inform on him. Since then, he tells us nothing,

though whispers come to us on occasion; Commander Nessus is

unwelcome among most of the herds now." Chiron exchanged glances

with Pholus, each understanding what the other was thinking. Nessus

had always been distrusted, though they did not share their suspicions

with the commanders. It was fortunate the herd leaders could discern

the manipulations of Nessus and both Chiron and Pholus felt justified

in their trust. Chiron was astonished at their independence of thought

and decision making; he had not checked in with the herd leaders in

millennia, and assumed they retained the intelligence he was

accustomed to. They were growing.

"Thank you for that, Commander," said Pholus. "We will deal with

Nessus later. For now, Master Chiron, please continue."

"Yes. Thank you," said Chiron. "As I stated, Aristotle has been imprisoned in the forbidden area cave. I wish to free him." Chiron looked at the faces of the herd leaders. They were blank and unemotional, and he could not read them, making him uncertain.

"I will assist you Master Chiron," said one of the leaders. And like a wave, he was joined by the entire group. Chiron's story had somehow emboldened them to fight against the demons, and each of them desired the glory of defeating one of the beasts. Like the battle with the harpies, it proved to be a greatly bonding summons to service. His people loved the thrill and adventure of battle.

"You honor all our kind with your loyalty and dedication, my friends. All can assist in some manner, though some will be less directly involved in the success of the operation. I did request Mortuus to join in our extraction, as the great teacher was the one who found and woke him from the eternal sleep. There is also a danger the Fallen may arrive, and he alone would be nearest their equal. I -"

"I will assist," interrupted Asterion, curt and assured, leaving no question of his involvement. Chiron, surprised, looked at Darius for a moment, cutting him off as he started to speak.

"No, Darius," said Chiron calmly. "This is no fight for humans. You will wait for us to bring Aristotle in the Wood." Darius conceded his agreement, understanding he would be the least effective in such a venture. He would be more than honored to help the legendary Aristotle, the sole reason he dared to cross from the Vestibule and the temporary safety of the rocky oasis in the first place. It had seemed so long ago that he and Mortuus colluded on crossing over the river Acheron together.

"I am happy to assist and hasten the regeneration, Lord Chiron. I have brought many vials of Limbo's waters." said Darius. Chiron smiled and nodded thankfully.

"Very well, then," he said. "We shall now make our plans to enter the forbidden area cave and extract Aristotle." And so they strategized, human, Fallen, and Halflings, working together for the first time.

It was an odd day in Hell.

Chapter 57

Reunification

Chiron and the commanders had been sitting and strategizing for some time before a member of Tacitus' herd approached. The commander excused himself, and trotted away with his subordinate, returning a short time later. In the distance, a trio of centaurs stood and talked with each other as a smaller figure walked around nearby. Chiron stopped talking with his commanders as he saw the human form in the distance.

"Tacitus. Why is there a human standing among your herd?" he asked.

"That human is a fugitive, captured by the harpies as he came through the Wood," replied Tacitus. "He was saved from the bird beasts, at the same site where we did battle with the harpies, but he had been so mutilated we could not communicate with him. He is just now regenerated enough to speak and his guard had thought this might be a good time for you to question him."

"Why are we keeping a fugitive?" asked Chiron. "Do we not usually just return them to the plain?"

"Yes, normally, Master Chiron. This one is different. He had the smell of the First Circle on him," Pholus chimed in.

"I requested we hold onto the fugitive until you could question him."

"He smells of the Vestibule?" asked Chiron. "I would like to ask him now, if I may interrupt our planning for a few minutes, commanders." And to this they all nodded. Tacitus galloped to his guards assigned to the human, then returned as they followed in the distance. The human was slower than they, and no centaur would dare allow a human to ride upon his back. Darius and Mortuus, who had been sitting on the outskirts of the meeting, stood and watched as the centaurs and human approached. Darius gasped as they neared.

"Panos!" he yelled. "Panos!" The centaur commanders and Chiron stared at him as he took off running. Chiron, fearful Darius might be attacked by the centaurs, who did not know him, trotted ahead of him quickly, and waved his arms to the centaur guard, who were just pulling their bows back.

"Stand down brave fellows," called Chiron. "He is a visitor here - not to be harmed." The centaurs bowed, acknowledging Chiron's wishes. The human, who had ran behind the centaur guards as Chiron came running at them looked sheepishly at the Master Centaur.

"I would speak to you as to your origins, but I have just determined who you are...Panos." Panos, overwhelmed by this, spoke but could only choke the words out. His voice was barely healed. His fear turned to joy as he saw Darius run up behind Chiron.

"Panos!" yelled Darius, now out of breath, but overjoyed at the sight of his friend. "You escaped once again!" The centaur guards watched the pair hug curiously. Centaur protocol did not permit bodily contact; it would have been considered a sign of weakness. Chiron continued his questioning.

"So this is Panos, of whom you spoke in the mine Darius. It seems his luck is great if he has escaped the flyer demons."

"How did you escape Panos?" asked Darius, still smiling. Panos tried to speak but could not. His throat had been ripped apart by the harpies. He gurgled some sounds, shrugged at the futility of it, then smiled again at his friend. He then placed his hands up, one with the fingers moving to look like wings flapping, and the other attached to the bottom, trying his best to show how he had been dropped from the flyer. Chiron understood.

"They dropped you? But why did they not retrieve you after? You surely were unable to run from them?" At this, Panos made motions with his hands again, and sounds that were near enough to the whooshing of the fireballs of the burning plain for Chiron to comprehend.

"Ah. The fireballs. Of course. The demons dropped you upon the burning plain, and so would not pursue you. The fireballs that fall there are quite intimidating. Although you must have suffered greatly, you were saved from being deposited into the deeper circles." Panos nodded.

"Very good for you, Panos. You were not aware of the harpies, unfortunately, but we shall remedy their damage for you shortly. Darius, take him back to where you and Mortuus are sitting. I believe we have enough vials to share some of the healing waters." The centaur guards, relieved to not have to watch the human fugitive any longer, returned to the greater herd across Phlegethon. Chiron returned to his meeting, resuming his planning with the commanders, as Darius and Panos strolled along. They had a lot to catch up on, and of course it would be Darius who spoke first, just after introducing his friend to his new friend, the angel Mortuus and Asterion, also known as the Minotaur.

Panos would have been stunned to silence even if he could speak.

Chapter 58

Secret Society No More

Benjamin walked the Hall of the Science in his search. In room after room, Benjamin walked in and out, asking those scientists attending the various botanical gardens, laboratories and meeting rooms, where he might find the senior scientist. Each person shrugged his shoulders or shook his head, then returned to the conversation or work he was previously engaged in. On the fourth floor, Benjamin got his answer from an apprentice of the senior scientist. Another man looked at the apprentice with disapproval. Benjamin was considered a pariah by many of these scientists, and this one was a known supporter of the Elders and their policies.

"He was just here moments ago." said the apprentice. "I believe I heard the roof door slam just now. You may check up there."

Benjamin headed toward the end of the fourth floor hallway and climbed up the small stairway to the open roof of the building. He looked around the roof looking for the senior scientist and found no one. Walking toward the edge of the building, he looked down and saw the small band of warriors standing there waiting. He waved his arms to get their attention, side to side, shrugged exaggeratedly with his arms, signaling that he did not find who he was looking for. Benjamin turned, looking toward the small, square shaped protrusion that led back to the stairs and down into the Hall of Science and was suddenly grabbed from the back of the shoulders, by hands that were like steel claws. The fingers with their sharp as talon nails gripped his shoulders so hard that they pierced his skin, drawing blood from under his robes. The pain caused Benjamin to scream. Up he was lifted, high off the roof, and out over the center of the small village huts below. He could make out the formation on the ground, watching him as he flopped like a fish on a hook, desperate to escape the pain. He looked up, and saw the creature that carried him, a demon, but wearing the clothing of the senior scientist. It was as he suspected. He began to breathe deeply, trying to alleviate the pain as he began to speak the words of the spell that would destroy the beast.

"Mmph!" The creature had been aware Benjamin was readying the spell, and covered his mouth, leaving him to dangle from only one clawed hand, more painful with his weight distributed from only one side. The beast's fingers penetrated Benjamin's face; so tight was its grip. It flew more precariously with the imbalance of weight.

"Where is the angel?!" hissed the creature, growling loudly. The two were flying lower, and the formation had disappeared from underneath. Benjamin was alone; this beast would rend him to pieces whether he talked or not. He shuddered, then braced himself, letting go of hope. "Where is it?!" hissed the former senior scientist. Benjamin would not answer. The creature began beating his wings faster, and began to climb up toward the misty ceiling that overhung Limbo. "Very well, Benjamin. You will need to think about it. I will let you keep your secret while you linger at the bottom of Acheron with the other fools."

They turned in the air, and Benjamin saw the Hall of Science building fly underneath him in the opposite direction, and then the wood behind the Hall. He would be sacrificed for Mortuus. He lost hope, just as the projectile thudded into his lower back. The sharp pain of the arrow caused him to scream as never before. The demon, startled by the arrow impact on his prey, turned them around in the air, just in time for Benjamin to see the hall with the company of warriors on its roof. The demon screeched indignation and pain, its own hide covered with several arrows in the wink of an eye.   Benjamin was dropped.

Militus, on the roof, yelled to his men again, and now the arrows rained

at the sky in a line toward the demon. It faltered and flew away from

the building, then tumbled down into the wood. With a crash, it struck

the trees, shrieking in pain. Benjamin had landed near the hall, a

sickening thud denoting his arrival on ground. He was laid flat on his

back, the wind knocked out of him, and most of his bones broken and

protruding through his skin or into his internal organs. The arrow had

pushed through on impact, and the point and shaft were protruding

from his belly as the fletching was inside his body.

It was only a minute before Militus and his soldiers came to the aid

of Benjamin. The men quickly produced several vials from the First

Waters and poured it into and on the broken body of the scientist. One

man pulled the arrow out as the broken scientist groaned loudly. Barely

able to move, Benjamin motioned toward where the demon had fallen

in the wood.

"Do not concern yourself, Benjamin. My men are hunters, and they

revel in the hunt as much as the battle. They are on its trail. Quiet

yourself for now, my friend. We will carry you to the healing waters

soon enough," assured Militus. Benjamin smiled weakly. Soon, a

soldier came up to Militus, spoke to him briefly, then left, joined by more of the soldiers who surrounded Benjamin. Benjamin did not know that the demon had somehow escaped the hunting party, wounded as he was. Militus looked worried as he turned back toward his friend, taking out another vial.

"Drink up. We will move soon. I'm sure the beast is making his way back to you. This one has lured away most of the men. Now drink." Each vial of cool water made Benjamin lose a bit of the pain, and so he forced himself to drink.

Moments later, there was a loud screech and the demon reappeared. It had made its way back around the wood, taking a long way in order to avoid the arrows of the soldiers. It came up, around the hall, surprising the soldiers who remained with Militus and Benjamin. They notched their arrows, pulled and loosed. But the creature was ready this time. It ducked behind a wide tree faster than they could see, then suddenly, it had climbed all the way up the tree, then flew and rammed into the soldiers. They were sent flying into a stand of smaller trees, two impaled coarsely on jagged branches sticking out. The other hit a tree with a thud, and was immobilized. The demon turned, and stared at Militus and Benjamin, pulling out the remaining arrows.

"Where is the angel!?!" it yelled at them in its low hissing voice. Militus walked toward the demon, and the demon stared at him as he approached. "This is not one of your foolish games, Militus," it hissed. The demon walked toward Militus, who was pulling out his sword. "You cannot destroy me." The demon watched as Militus flexed his wrist, swooshing with the sword as if warming up for a fight, much as an athlete would stretch before a tournament event. The demon, disdainfully curious, watched the flicks. "What are you doing, Militus?" asked the creature. "Am I to be frightened by your display?" The demon pulled out the last arrow, and Benjamin, despite his pain, sat up enough to look at Militus, puzzled. Militus smiled, and the demon seemed to portray a curious look on its deformed face.

"You are a slow thinker, imp." Militus was poking at the demon's ego, and the demon became visibly enraged. "I am only buying time," confessed Militus. And with that, the demon flinched and screeched in pain as it was struck with arrow after arrow from behind, it's back filled with feathery shafts. It fell to the ground screeching, and before it could get up, the soldiers who had been tracking it appeared out of the tree line. The beast stretched its wings, trying to push up from the ground. The soldiers pinned the wings with spears and swords, and sat on the beast to keep it still. They steered clear of the legs. Militus moved next to it, and sat down on the ground near its head. It gnashed and cursed him repeatedly. When the beast finally calmed and glared in exhaustion, Militus questioned it.

"How many of you reside within Limbo, demon, and where?" asked Militus. The beast cursed more, and when it grew tired of cursing Militus, it quieted, only to be aroused in pain by the soldiers standing on its shoulder and wings. It was a long interrogation, and when Militus determined he would get no more than the few answers from the beast, the demon was placed into a choke hold by the largest of his men. It took a long time, as it did for the Elder demon destroyed by Mortuus, before the beast smoked, a black cloud denoting its former state. The strangling warrior was cheered by his fellows. The men picked up their arrows and departed to recover at the First Waters, carrying along Benjamin and the others disabled in the encounter. Various scientists who were within the Hall watching the situation moved away from their windows, trying to be unseen by the soldiers and Militus.

Benjamin and Militus sat near a tree on the edge of the stream bank. Soon, they were joined by Barak, Socius, and Alcander, who was in chains, Alcander's two guards, and Clavius.

"The Society is no more," said Benjamin. "We just had a *talk* with our old friend, the senior scientist. You were correct Clavius, he was a demon." Socius winced, and Clavius shook his head. "The infiltration by these demons is deep. They are among the Society members."

"Why do they come here?" asked Socius. "What are they watching us for? Mortuus has not been that long escaped from the underground sleep. They have been here far longer."

"They watch us for their Fallen masters" answered Benjamin grimly. "Though you may not have gathered this, we are prisoners in a gilded cage, and we must be kept under control. At least as far as they are concerned. They know we helped the angel to escape, and it will not be long before they appear. I am afraid we may be sent to the outside." The idea of being placed outside of Limbo's pleasant environs weighed upon all of them.

"I am troubled by this possibility also," Militus stated frankly.

"Why do the Fallen not come and find Mortuus themselves," asked Socius.

"Fallen would not bother with our lot," said Clavius. "We are insects in their eyes, and they would rather train their demon dogs to keep us in line than dirty their hands. Since we threaten the established order, we may have severe consequences. There is only one who can help us at this point. We must go to the Chronicler."

Barak looked at the group. He was the most loyal and dedicated follower of the Chronicler, and even he would be allowed to see the secluded teacher only on the rarest of occasions. But they were in need, desperately, and the answers could only come from the Chronicler. Barak nodded his head.

"Very well. I will take you, and we can try for an audience. Drink up. It is a very long walk, and we shall need to watch much more carefully for the beasts. They will be hunting for us this time."
Barak started to fill vials from the stream, and secretly wished, for a split second, that Aristotle had never woken Mortuus.

Chapter 59

Nessus and the Centaur Rebellion

The band of centaurs, the angel Mortuus and the human Darius had gathered outside of the cave, as close as they dared prior to making known their intention. The planning for this event had been successful: many centaurs had volunteered, far more than could fit into the cave mouth, and so Chiron had proposed that the remaining herd could spread out, making a warning system to indicate the Fallen approaching from anywhere around the seventh circle. Across the river from the cave, the herds had also formed a line of a score of meters apart.

The imps of the forbidden area cave, seeing the crowding centaurs in the nearer distance, on both sides of the cave, watched and hissed and shrank back into the large dark opening. Chiron waited, watching as the numbers of centaurs increased by the minute. He was as a proud father, but wary that taking his herds into so much danger would hurt the race of centaurs and their morality forever after if their fight was unsuccessful. And, by all accounts of the powers of the Fallen and their demons, there was no reason to believe this fight could have a good ending for any of the rebels. Chiron was flanked by Asterion, who was shadowing the Master Centaur more as time passed.

Asterion was still, but his large bull eyes darted back and forth, nervously, feeling all but swallowed in the sea of centaurs. Asterion had only one friend during his harsh lifetime, a servant child who, in her naïveté, did not fear him; but she had been taken from him when their friendship was discovered and reported to the guards. Her removal from his life was a cruelty in itself, and the advisor to the King made certain to beat the child severely where her cries could be heard by Asterion. It had caused the tortured half-bull the most pain and rage, and his full hatred of humans came to a pinnacle at that point in his life. Now he had a friend again, but his joy was mottled with his insecurity in this large crowd. The best he could do was to stand still and wait for the battle to start, calming himself with deep breaths, which made him appear to be angry. It did not help that the centaurs stared so intensely. They had been briefed by their commanders about Asterion, and many were curious and wished to approach their newest fellow Halfling. His bull-countenance was far too foreboding, and they were preparing for the fight of their afterlives. Fellowship would have to wait.

Darius and Mortuus stood behind Chiron and Asterion, each in a frightened anticipation for the battle to come. Panos was strutting about nervously too, as several of the younger centaurs watched. One centaur mouthed the words "filthy human coward" to his fellows, wishing to grasp the fearful, pacing human and toss him into the boiling river. This circle's centaurs could tolerate humans, but had absolutely no threshold for fear. Panos, in his state of worry, was unaware of anyone's current views and judgments. He knew fear. It was all he could do not to turn and run away. Were it not for the presence of Darius, Panos would have scurried away hastily and been up the rocky slope heading toward the First Circle. The centaurs, disgusted, turned and talked among themselves, distracting themselves with the coming glory of battle which they heavily anticipated.

Pholus was behind, watching as the centaurs strutted toward Chiron. He would be the last to enter the cave mouth. As he watched the last of them arrive, Pholus noted another formation, coming up slowly, moving very uniformly. Thinking that they were a proud company, he smiled. But Chiron did not. His inner eye had begun another vision, and he appeared to stare into space blankly.

The centaurs were shooting at each other, and those wounded were attacked by the harpies, who shredded them easily in their wounded state; Chiron saw a leader, smiling as he pulled his bow and shot the arrows into his fellow centaurs, then hefted them into the red river, cursing them loudly. The leader was familiar, but Chiron could not make out his face. The Master Centaur stepped forward in his vision, just to the edge of sight and the vision faded.

Chiron returned to consciousness, and suddenly motioned Pholus and the company nearest him to assume an attack formation. The alarm in Chiron's voice caused the centaur companies to move quickly, quieting them immediately. The silence and formation occurred speedily, as Chiron looked to and fro for his foreseen nemesis. Mortuus, Darius and Asterion followed the movements of Chiron, but he waved them to stay put as he addressed the herds.

"My fellows," Chiron called, "We are betrayed by our own. Turn and look behind you. And prepare for battle." Chiron trotted toward what was now the front line of the centaurs, who, although puzzled, followed their chief commander to a fault. Seeing the large company of centaurs drawing near, they readied themselves. It was clear this regiment would easily have come up from behind had Chiron not had his vision. Pholus, the closest to the oncoming centaurs, began cursing loudly. Chiron's suspicions were confirmed.

Nessus was the leader of the opposing force in his vision.

Nessus shouted to the company to halt, and approached Chiron and Pholus, both of whom had moved between the companies. The two had only moved a short distance from their company, causing Nessus to move far from his standing company. Chiron stared at Pholus, and then winked. It was then Pholus knew that his old friend was up to something.

"Master. I have grave news." Nessus began, "The Fallen know of your plans to enter the forbidden area cave. They will arrive any moment. I fear you will be removed from your post, along with Master Pholus." Chiron and Pholus were in a state of false shock, playing to Nessus' lies and treachery, yet still somewhat astonished that this fool of a centaur had performed the ultimate act of treachery and sided with the Fallen.

"And how did they learn of our undertaking, Nessus?" Pholus stabbed his words at Nessus, because he knew the answer already.

"I told them," said Nessus, calm and cold. Pholus was enraged, his anger grown to violent proportion. Chiron, however, remained calm, and motioned Pholus to stand down. The company of centaurs behind

Nessus were ready to battle, and the company brought up by Pholus

began their stance. Chiron smiled and waved to all the centaurs, and

they returned his greeting with bows. Suddenly, the Master Centaur

began to shout, talking loudly for both opposing companies to hear

him. The face of Nessus was a question.

"YOU WOULD CHALLENGE ME THEN NESSUS, FOR THE

MANTLE OF LEADERSHIP? I ACCEPT!" The herds on both sides

began their cheering, as they had so long ago when Chiron was

challenged before. Brutus had fulfilled his penance after challenging

and losing to his leader. Now the herds would witness Chiron against

Nessus. No one would fight today except these two warriors. Chiron

had sidestepped Nessus' attempted overthrow with a shout.

Nessus almost collapsed at his self-inflicted misfortune, reeling at

his easy loss. He knew he was no match at all against the Master

Centaur. Chiron had tricked him into moving out of hearing range of

his company, and then issued the challenge. Centaurs could not call

their kind to help in the challenge for leadership; it was against their

code of honor. Even the traitorous centaurs would not abandon this

code in the face of the larger herds. Nessus, his dreams of power destroyed, galloped and jumped into the boiling river rather than waiting to be thrown in. His screams faded as he moved away, swimming to complete his five rounds, the prescribed punishment for the loser of the challenge. Adding to his pride's injury, the humans who inhabited the river watched as Nessus swam among them.

The rebellion was over before its start. Chiron saw the harpies in the background, circling quietly in the air, and watching the centaur companies. The harpies rarely ever traveled to this side of Phlegethon, and their presence indicated that Nessus had made what had to be a pretty good deal with them, as their loathing of the Fallen and the allies of the Fallen were great. The company who came with Nessus dispersed, puzzled, and returned to their former posts, never knowing why Nessus had promised them glorious battle. Nessus had sought out the least intelligent and the most easily misguided members of the herds and recruited them over a long period of time, promising them commander status and glory if they would fight against the oppression that Chiron had put upon the herds; and mentioning many times Chiron's secret dealings with their greatest enemies, the humans. Their surprise at his sudden decision to challenge the Master Centaur was great, and their disappointment greater. Nessus had cowered in dishonor, and thus humiliated, could never again be recognized or respected as any sort of leader of the herds. To have placed their trust in such a leader would cause them misery for the rest of their stay in Hell, and none were too dimwitted or misguided to miss that single, cogent fact.

Chiron questioned the second in command of Nessus' company, who told him Nessus had setup a lone centaur to stand ready to blow the horn that would summon the Fallen. This centaur had luckily not blown the horn, because Nessus' command never came. Pholus retrieved the horn, placing it in the safekeeping of Commander Tacitus. Nessus' Second in Command insisted he knew no more and several of the trusted centaur commanders agreed he was probably telling the truth, verifying the centaurs' lack of intelligence in general. Chiron and Pholus speculated that Nessus would have informed the Fallen of Chiron's intent to enter the cave after the battle was complete, thus granting the traitor the role of leader of the centaurs. The scale of the treachery was unbelievably foolish, even for Nessus.

"Fool! Traitor! What will you do with him and his traitors?" asked Pholus.

"I do not know but I will have decided something by the time he is finished his rounds." returned Chiron.

"Now to our task."

Chapter 60

Inside the Cave

The battle was no more than a few minutes long. The centaurs, directed by Chiron to surround the cave entrance, watched for Fallen or their demon counterparts in the air above. Not a single creature was sighted beyond the few imps who were always present. Chiron, along with Mortuus, Asterion and Pholus went into the cave first. Darius and Panos were sent across the river to a hiding place within the Wood. The pair of humans were carried across the boiling river by Titan, the youthful centaur who was the least affronted by their riding upon his back.

Many centaurs, aroused for a grand battle, were disappointed at the prospect of being mere lookouts, but Pholus reminded them of the power of the Fallen, and the threat if they were to arrive suddenly. Still, they could not understand why the 'human' Mortuus was allowed to enter, along with the Minotaur. Chiron and the commanders decided to keep Mortuus' identity a secret for the time being; the Fallen were the unmistakable grand lords of Hell, undefeatable. This reputation would surely cause his kind to size up and attempted to challenge Mortuus' status as Fallen. Chiron's people were not shy to challenge power, and he did not feel they were ready to understand an alliance with one of their jailers.

The small imps loitering at the outside of the cave shrunk back inside at the sight of the approaching party, hissing and growling. The odd company of centaur, minotaur and angel approached the cave warily, ready for anything. A handful of imps, between the size of demons and imps, had been waiting at the entrance, just back in the shadow. They jumped out suddenly and startled the company. Before Chiron and Pholus could turn them into screaming smoke, a score of arrows whooshed by their ears and into the beasts within seconds. Mortuus stood, in shocked awe as the two mighty centaurs looked around. The lookouts, eager for battle, had unleashed their projectiles from far away at the sight of the creatures. Chiron and Pholus glared at the lookout centaurs sternly.

"Do not draw your bows again. You are to keep watch only!" yelled Pholus. A distant commander replied.

"Apologies, Master Chiron and Master Pholus," he said, embarrassed.

The guard imps had no chance. Falling down in pain, they writhed for a moment with several arrows protruding from each of them. Asterion, newly equipped by the centaurs with a large spear, wasted no time and finished them off. The entrance became a smoking barrel, and Chiron and Pholus collected the arrows from the ground to leave as little trace of their visit as possible.

There was little light inside the carved hallway going into the first chamber of the cave. Chiron and Pholus struggled to see ahead in vain, but Mortuus saw the danger ahead easily.

"Chiron, Pholus – aim where I point. There, straight ahead!" said Mortuus. The two needed no prodding. Their arrows thudded into something, and the screeches which followed were deafening in the cave acoustics. Mortuus ran ahead, followed by Asterion. A loud pop followed as Mortuus and Asterion stabbed at the ground. Another imp dissipated. The company entered the inner chamber.

It was a large compartment, and the smell and look reminded Mortuus uncomfortably of his recent origin. Two sets of doorways, covered with heavy wrought iron bars were placed at the far sides of the room, both on the left and the right of a flat, back wall, made of solid black rock. Behind the bars were stairways, carved into the rock, leading upward and out of sight. This inner cavern was lit more brightly, like Clavius' hallway in Porto. Mortuus surmised the same magic was used to create the light. An ancient, ornately carved table next to the left wall held a large opened book. It was the only furniture they found in this strange cavity. Behind the table and against the wall, a fine, filthy old cloth veiled a large rectangular area. Chiron went to the cloth and pushed it aside cautiously. Behind the cloth was a dusty mirror, a duplicate of one in the Hall of Minos. He quickly released the cloth and it fluttered back to its former position covering the silvered glass. Chiron did not wish to trigger the mirror if it had the same magical teleportation function as Minos' mirror of judgment. Everyone watched as he moved back from the wall.

"Stay away from this - all of you. I will explain later..." No one in the room had ever seen the mirror of Minos; it was only used to judge humans. The two centaurs, Chiron and Pholus, searched the room and found near the barred doorways, levers jutting out from the walls.

"Try the lever on the right, Mortuus," said Chiron. "Though cautiously..." In a moment Mortuus had pulled the switch, and opened the right gateway. "This way friends." They followed Chiron, as the stairway was fit only for one centaur at a time. A short climb later, they were at the top of the steps, and Mortuus started to feel claustrophobic again. He recalled his hellish awakening, and his journey through the mines with Eruos. Angels must not be accustomed to caves, he thought. He swallowed hard, determined to get past his fear, and kept walking. The hallway at the top abruptly turned right, and the group followed Chiron further into the rocky structure.

Mortuus noticed something suddenly. As they walked, an entrance appeared on the left of the hall. It was closed but nevertheless there. He stopped, looking at the shape of this doorway. It reminded him of the first demon he had found in Limbo, hidden by magical means. It phased in and out of his vision, a surreal, gossamer veil appearing as rock, then door opening. He decided to check his theory.

"Chiron – stop for a moment. Asterion, Pholus – look at this wall. Do you see anything strange about it?" asked Mortuus.

"I see nothing but rock." returned Pholus. Chiron and Asterion nodded in agreement.

"Then only I am seeing this," said Mortuus. "Pholus, please help me to push, here." Mortuus showed Pholus where to put his hands, and struggled as they pushed into the wall. Chiron started to look around the wall, for any sort of device that would have helped open the doorway. Asterion had his own ideas. He began to brutally butt the wall with his head, hoping that his rage driven strength would open a passage. It did nothing. Then, Mortuus, looking directly across from the phasing doorway saw it. A small lever, a miniature version of those that opened the bars at the base of the steps, was hidden just like the doorway. Mortuus grabbed the lever cautiously.

"Watch my friends." Mortuus pulled the lever and the hallway wall opened. The four walked inside a low-ceilinged room, barely higher than the centaurs.

Chiron saw them first; on a single carved rock table, three large gems, looking polished and perfectly cut. They were each the size of a human heart, and two were clear, sparkling like diamonds. The other was a deep crystalline blue, giving off a slight glow that seemed to brighten as they neared it. Mortuus looked closely at the stones, stunned. His memory stirred in the darkness, but he was still disconnected from it. Instinctively, he knew he needed to take the blue glowing gem. Almost involuntarily, Mortuus reached for the stone and, holding it gently, caressed it as if it were a dear pet. For a moment he thought of Socius, and did not know why. The gem glowed more brightly and the glow fluttered, then subsided back to its' original radiance. Mortuus placed the stone into his pack gingerly as Chiron and Pholus watched.

"What is this stone, Mortuus?" asked Chiron. "You seem as if you have found something dear. Precious gems mean nothing here. Do you have a recollection?"

"No," said Mortuus, "But I am compelled to take it. If I can trust my feelings to be correct, this is a living creature, though I know not what. My heart would suffer to leave it in the hands of these despicable Fallen, though I have no other explanation to offer."

"That explanation will do for now. And what of the other, clear gems?" asked Chiron.

"When I look at them, I feel great sadness. They are brilliant, but empty, unlike this one. My memory has been stirred, though not yet enough." Chiron nodded.

"I will take these two also." said Chiron, placing them into his pack. "We will get our answers later. If these are so guarded, the Fallen must place some value in them. I believe your memory will return, and when it does, we shall have many answers. For now, we shall have to be patient."

181

"Hurry friends. We delay too long and I have concern the Fallen will find us within," interrupted Pholus. Asterion grunted agreement as he rubbed his sore head. The intruders resumed their path up the hallway, which climbed to another set of stairs that wound left, then ended in a large, long room. Large stone slab tables lay in the middle of the room, and another table on the far wall was pressed into the corner. On the floor was a bloodied, ripped robe, a once fine garment crafted by the weavers of Porto. Chiron and Pholus recognized the colors and patterns immediately; this robe had been given to Aristotle many centuries ago.

Within seconds the group assessed the room. Two tables, those nearest the entryway, had multiple sharp spikes protruding from their surfaces. Over the tables, a flat stone was suspended by chains attached to the top of the room, with holes in the underside directly corresponding to the spikes coming out of the table beneath the hanging rock. The chains holding the stones up were attached to a single chain, in turn attached to a sophisticated gear system next to a lever. The levers of the first two tables were up, but the third table lever was down; the flat stone slab, with chains piled on it, gripped them all as, coming out from between the two stones, a slow trickle of blood made a tiny stream onto the filthy rock floor.

They had found Aristotle.

"Quickly!" motioned Chiron, "Pull that lever Pholus!" The group surrounded the table, and the stones began to slowly part, as Pholus struggled to push up the lever switch. Asterion, seeing the efforts of the centaur were not enough, placed his giant hand over the centaurs', and the lever moved up almost effortlessly. They watched horrified, seeing the great teacher, the explorer, the awakener of angels, in this most hideous form, crushed, bleeding, mangled; unrecognizable. Chiron wept and Mortuus stood quietly as the leader of the centaurs covered his eyes.

"Ugh," came and unguarded sound from Pholus. He shook his large head at the mangled mass of flesh that was Aristotle. "Shall I use some of the remaining vials, Chiron?"

"If you have them use them," replied Chiron, "just do it quickly." Pholus opened up his pack, moving some small items out of the way. From its bottom, he pulled out the last three small vials of the waters packaged from Limbo.

"Mystical, I would say," said Pholus, "that the teacher was so generous with the healing waters that will begin his own restoration. I am beginning to feel hope for some reason." Asterion looked as Pholus spoke, and said nothing. He stared at Aristotle's mutilated form, and swore curses at the Fallen who would do such a thing to anyone.

"Pour the waters on his midsection, Pholus," directed Chiron, "The healing will be best begin there. I will administer one onto the head and neck. We will transport him as soon as we can. The longer we stay here the more peril we are in."

It was a relatively long time before they were able to move Aristotle's body. As soon as he was able to groan in an audible tone, the pair of centaurs picked him up and placed him into the arms of Mortuus. The blood and gore were almost too much for Mortuus to bear, but he put aside his revulsion as best as he could. The human who had awakened him would not suffer long as far as Mortuus was concerned. Chiron led as the search party left the torture chamber behind. They went back to the large room at the opening, when Mortuus thought he had heard Aristotle speak.

"Wait, Chiron, Pholus. Aristotle has said something. I cannot discern it. Come closer, maybe one of you can make out his words."

184

The bloody gore that was Aristotle moved something that had once been his jaw. The centaurs bent closer, but heard only a light muttering of pain. Asterion bent near, and the rescuers tensed up in concentration.

"Other," said Asterion. "Other. He has asked to get another." Chiron looked intensely around the room, searching for some clue as to what Aristotle was talking about. "Perhaps he is just in too much pain," said the half-bull.

"No. I have known this human for many centuries. I believe we may have to go into that other entrance. Mortuus - take Aristotle out of this place. Have one of the commanders escort you to where Darius remains hidden in the Wood, awaiting our return with Aristotle. They will lead you to the rill, under the tree covering. You and Aristotle are who the Fallen will be searching for, so remain hidden until I arrive. Farewell if I do not see you again. You have given me new respect, and hope, for angel kind." Mortuus was moved by Chiron's words, and turned to exit the cave.

Upon exiting the cave, Mortuus was met by a company of centaurs who had been waiting to take him and Aristotle to the Wood. But the centaurs were reluctant to carry Mortuus and the bloody pulp that was Aristotle across the river, so Mortuus began walking across at the rivers shallowest point. The centaurs stood in disbelief that Mortuus did not falter, and insisted that he wait and they would call for Titan to carry the pair across. Mortuus continued walking, grimacing with each step. The burning on his feet was worse than he had imagined, and he nearly dropped Aristotle. The river seemed wide here, but he could see that it was just his imagination. The pain intensified, and was unbearable, and Mortuus began to running as he neared the bank on the other side, collapsing awkwardly into a small heap, still holding his damaged, dear awakener. Aristotle's moaning grew louder, prompting Mortuus to stand again on his burnt feet. The centaurs led the way. They reached the trees much later, and were soon met by Pholus, Asterion and Chiron, who were carrying another gory inhabitant from the cave whom they found in the other room Aristotle mentioned. This one had had no water sprinkled on his wounds, and was as quiet as death. He looked quite horrific and moldy, as if he had been there a very long time.

"We will need to conserve the waters for this one." said Chiron. "I want to know why he was being kept hidden by the Fallen. He has been there much longer than Aristotle. Do you see how his wounds have tried to heal in such a strange manner? His legs seem to have grown back together with holes in them."

"Aye - and his blood hardly flowed away from the table." added Pholus. "I do not think he will be able to speak for quite awhile."

"We will first heal Aristotle, and find out why he wanted to save this one," said Chiron. "I do not believe he is angel."

"Nor do I Chiron," said Mortuus apprehensively. "I see no magical energy flowing in him. He might just be a very troublesome fugitive to the Fallen. I wonder what kind of secrets he knows to get such special treatment?"

"He is no mere fugitive to receive this treatment, Mortuus," said Chiron, changing his mind. "Plutus was a troublesome wanderer, and he had no such punishment. This one has truly incurred their wrath and fear. I will get my waters and return shortly. Both will need to be regenerated promptly. Where is Darius? We can also use his water." Chiron left, and returned shortly with a few more vials of waters. Behind him were Darius and Panos, both having followed the centaurs rather than staying alone with the harpies of the Wood. Darius gave up his water without hesitation, as did Mortuus, and between them the pair of crushed corpses that were Aristotle and the stranger regenerated greatly.

Despite their efforts, it still turned out to be a long wait.

Chapter 61

The Chronicler

The band arrived at the Chronicler's cottage in small fragments. They had decided to travel in packs of three, dividing themselves up to not arouse suspicion. They also had grown by two when they left the mine. Barak, Socius and Militus went in the first group and were followed by Benjamin, who was cloaked because of his high profile in the scientific community, along with the two miners Abreo and Exaro, who were insistent on traveling with the group. Eruo remained behind in order to handle the worker demons who might be coming for more ore, thereby deflecting any suspicion from the mine area.

Behind Benjamin and the miners were the warriors, who had been accompanying the group, split into many groups of three. Militus had seen to the hiding of Alcander deep within the mines, two of the warriors guarding him in a hidden wing. Clavius had volunteered his laboratory for holding the corrupt Elder, but Socius and Militus balked at this suggestion. Clavius stayed behind in Porto, arranging his cottage to appear more like his neighbors in the odd case that it was searched.

189

The walk was long. The Chronicler's cottage was near the far wall of Limbo, almost a complete circle from the entrance to Limbo. Many citizens of Limbo had requested the Elders to petition the Fallen for an entrance way across the path that ran through the Second Circle, and had been refused by the Elders, who stated the Fallen wanted only one entrance into and out of Limbo. The petitioners objected strenuously, but the Fallen were quite immovable.

When they had reached the cottage, they found several groups of students outside, sitting and apparently talking as they waited for the Chronicler. Barak knew many of the students, and walked over to ask his familiars as to the whereabouts of the Chronicler. Meanwhile, Socius and Militus sat down on the grass, waiting to see their trio of companions come along the path soon after. Socius began to have a conversation with Militus while they sat waiting. The grass was cool to sit upon, and the trees in the distance, known as the End Forest, were invitingly beautiful in their soft greenness, some with a silvery brilliance.

"Have you been here before Militus," asked Socius "I mean, to visit the Chronicler, or just to travel somewhere different?"

"I have," answered Militus, "though I have not been back here in ages. The Elysian fields are where I feel most at home, but this traveling we have done of late has stirred me to do more and see more. Do you see those trees in the distance?" Militus pointed toward the End Forest. "They were not here the last time I ventured out this far. It must be the Chronicler's doing. Behind the trees, hidden well, is the far wall to Limbo, across the path from the gateway. It's a wonder that no opening has been built there – we would surely see this part of Limbo more often."

"The work of the Elders, I'm sure," replied Socius, "Bureaucrats for the Fallen." Socius was bitter, angry at the injustice of those whom he understood to rule by fear, the ones who betrayed Aristotle. "Militus, are the Fallen so strong that we can never come up against them?"

"The Fallen are the most powerful beings in Hell. As far as we know, Hell was created for them to rule. They are cast out of their domain, but no one knows why, only that they were given rulership over Hell to mock them. But save your questions for the Chronicler; he will surely know more than I. Ahh – Barak is returning." Barak walked toward them, his face the picture of concern. Socius and Militus saw it immediately, and their hearts dropped as they anticipated grim news.

"We must go, there is danger here. I know most of these people, but they treat me as a stranger, as if I had *not* known them for centuries. We have to leave before our friends arrive. These impersonators claim not to have seen the Chronicler. I was going to press them with questions they should have been able to answer but thought better of it." Socius was looking beyond Barak at the small groups that were sitting on the ground, all eyes glaring at Militus, Barak and himself.

"Oh. Quickly then. Do not turn around Militus, just start walking back the way we came." As the youth looked, the grim gathering seemed to waver, as if a shimmering heat was rising off the ground and distorting them in the distance. The youth squinted, and then looked again. The watching mass was normal, so he decided his eyes were playing tricks on him in his alerted state. Then he saw it - they were walking toward the three. "Hold. They're moving toward us. Pretend we are not aware they are – different. Try to look normal." Militus put on a false smile, one he had used during his life dealing with politicians and his military superiors, and turned toward the cottage and the mob that formed. Barak pretended to talk to him, peripherally looking at the crowd, and when the pack moved nearer the three, they stood, as if to greet, and have Barak introduce them.

"We cannot destroy this many when we drop at the first casting of the spell," whispered Militus. "We will have to run."

"Play the fool my friends – they have no reason to suspect we know anything" replied Barak.

"What if they try to replace us with their fellow demons?" whispered Socius.

"We shall have to improvise as we go along," said Militus. The group surrounded them, appearing to be quite menacing. Barak addressed one of them, who looked in appearance like a very old friend of his, and started to introduce Militus and Socius, playing the friendly host as best he could to keep his countenance steady.

In the blink of an eye, Barak was flying backward, the victim of a sudden forcible backhand by his old 'friend.' Militus made to move into the man when he was suddenly picked up from behind and tossed into a stone pile not far from where they stood. His leg was broken and the wind knocked out of him, and he could not get to his feet. Socius fared the best, ducking reflexively as two of the men tried to grab his arms.

More of the masked demon assembly tried grabbing Socius, and he evaded very well, moving to keep out of their clawing grip, instinctively dodging their clawed hands as they tried to latch on to him. Pulling out his long knife, Socius waved it in front of several of them, trying to discourage them. Growling, they began reverting to their true forms; demons of many shapes and sizes, winged and not. In a moment he was underneath the swarm of these vile creatures, thrashing for his freedom, and damaging them as best he could. It was all he could do to utter the words of the spell. He would take out at least one of them before they ripped him apart. Before he could utter the spell, at the last moment, loud screams and screeching, intense heat, and the filthy stink of the beasts smoking were his universe, and then, he was no longer under a pile of demons.

Socius got to his feet, slowly, choking on the foul smoky air. He had been slashed and bitten on his legs, and his robes were ripped and shredded; his eyes were irritated by the stream of blood dripping from cuts and scratches on his forehead. He looked around and saw Barak, moaning as he slowly, painfully, got to his feet. He had stood up and limped slowly, leaving a bloody trail to mark his path. Militus was gone, as were the demons. All the demons. Socius, puzzled and afraid, ran to Barak to assist him. Socius could see out of the corner of his eyes, coming from the cottage, a man. He was moving in their direction. He waved his weapon at the figure and in a blink of the eye the man appeared next to Socius. The startled youth barely kept his wits, and though afraid, aimed his hostility at the man.

"Where is Militus?" yelled Socius. The large man, cloaked in a robe that looked as if it had been worn in outer hell many, many times, stared at Socius, examining him, seeming to scan his body, and then - smiling. Socius noted a gleam in the man's eyes of friendliness and warmth, behind a serious, mature, yet boyish face. The man, to Socius' surprise, began to help the stunned Barak to his feet.

"The demons have taken your commander Militus, Barak." said the cloaked man. "Come - I have healing potions that will have you and the boy as good as new." Barak smiled feebly at the man. "Let us walk to my cottage."

"Thank you master," said Barak. "I was afraid they had impersonated you as well." A new understanding swept over Socius. This was the Chronicler himself.

"Do not worry yourself, Barak," said the Chronicler, "And this, finally, is the one who you told me of, the babe delivered so long ago?"

"I would have to say yes by the way he dodged the demons." Barak smiled and motioned to Socius. "I am sorry to have waited so long to assist you, Socius. I only just arrived."

"Yes, it was he who came to Limbo as a child, and grew up among the warriors and teachers. Socius, I would like to introduce Master Avius, whom you know as the Chronicler." Socius smiled – here was the Chronicler himself, known to give an audience only once a century, standing with him and Barak.

"Brilliant," said Socius excitedly, "I am honored sir –" They were approaching the cottage entryway, where none entered, except the highest followers of the Chronicler, and very rarely. Barak had told Socius he could count the number of times he had entered the cottage on one hand, and each time the interior had been entirely different. "We are entering, Master Chronicler?" he asked respectfully. Aristotle had taught him good manners.

"Yes Socius – we are going inside. Welcome to my cottage. Please pardon my messiness - I have not cleaned in centuries." They walked inside, and found the interior was not much to look at, especially for someone so highly revered. Bare furniture, covered in dust, a table, a wooden floor, a large mirror, candles on the walls for light and some simple stones were all that Socius could see. It was a plainly normal interior. "Wait," said Avius and he turned to close the door behind them, then secure it with several large boards across the top, middle and bottom. He stepped over to a wall and tilted a candle holder that was tipped slightly sideways. Walking to the other side of the room, he did the same to another candle. In a moment, the mirror began to brighten, emitting a strong light around its edges, and the walls became stony, replacing the previous wood and thatch. The door behind them disappeared and was also replaced by a wall of stone. The room was, in a moment, far larger. Socius looked at Barak, who smiled through his bruises at Socius, who stood with his mouth agape. Avius returned to the side of Barak, and the three walked toward the mirror. It grew wide as they approached.

"Do not fear, Socius. Barak, you have told no one of this?" asked Avius.

"No one Master Avius," returned Barak. "Socius, you are the only other person in Limbo to enter this place."

And all at the same time, they walked, disappearing into the mirror of the Chronicler

Chapter 62

The Flight of Militus

Militus was screaming in pain. He was being carried, like prey caught and stretched between two large hawks. Strong claw-hands held him so tightly that they were causing him to bruise, and would have penetrated his skin were it not for his thick robes. They had picked him up from the rock pile and flown off, up into the air, transforming into demons in a split second, just as he had seen before with Alcander's Elder, the demon who was Morpheus.

He could see the ground falling away slowly as the creatures flew their hardest to lift his flailing weight. They did not see that they were flying over a group of three men, each with jaws agape in surprised horror. A great flash lit up the mist above Militus and the demons carrying him, as multiple shrieks assaulted their ears. the flash came from the field outside the house of the Chronicler. The demons screeched in angry surprise, and flew lower to inspect the scene they had just left.

Three of Militus' warriors, who had earlier grouped by threes to avoid suspicion as they traveled, had their bows pulled back, and aimed. They had seen the flash moments before and immediately readied for whatever was next. All at once, they loosed their arrows. The demons faltered, as two arrows pierced one of them. The last shaft missed its mark. The wounded demon, arrow shaft sticking from his gut and free shoulder, let loose Militus as the pain disabled and enraged him. Pulling the arrows out in irritation, the wounded demon screeched at the soldiers below while the other demon sank nearer the ground with the full weight of Militus. Not willing to endure more pain, the injured demon flew away, out of reach of the arrows. The demon still carrying Militus, soared upwards, joining his peer. Militus could hear them, speaking to each other in their coarse, barely understandable voices.

"I must regenerate. Take him to the pitch and throw him to the devils. Return here and we shall punish their impudence." The demon carrying Militus growled in agreement.

"Miserable, filthy humans."

"I will inform the masters of this. The humans had help. That was strong magic. Go now, and return when he is in the devil's care." And with that they split up, the demon carrying Militus rising high up, high enough to see the wall coming at them, and at the last moment, flying over the wall.

Militus decided to stop struggling and use his energy to assess an escape plan. The creature had in its belt a long knife and meat hook; Militus briefly remembered the description of how Darius' friends had been hauled off, and was thankful not to be dancing on the end of one of the hooks. He would wait for the right moment, and make his move. The pain of his broken leg was hardly bearable, but Militus had no choice but to hold onto his wits.

The demon and his cargo flew very close to the wall of Limbo and it seemed as if Militus would be smashed into it. At the last minute, the demon lifted higher. Militus watched the ground below. He could see they were just below the misty ceiling. His nose was suddenly assailed, as the smells of outer Hell reminded him of the terror he had experienced when he had first entered Hell, before being sent to Limbo by the mirror.

His memory flashback was interrupted, when below him, just appearing, were people who were floating, it appeared, or hovering, before suddenly being smashed into the wall that enclosed Limbo. The people would fall downward only to be picked up again and tossed around violently. The wind was the cruel torturer of these damned. Militus looked left and right, and everywhere below him were people being tossed against the wall.

The demon remained very high up, hugging the dark gray ceiling for a short while, and then, as the ground dipped, indicating the next circle, began to descend.

In the next circle, Militus could smell the putrid smell of rotten food, vomit, and long decayed flesh and blood. The flight continued down to the next circle, and now the ground was full of groups of people, frantically pushing large boulders at each other, the sound of the boulders hitting loudly, booming up enough for Militus to hear. Further down they flew, the demon and his prey, towards the bowels of Hell.

Another cliff indicated the next circle, and the ground became suddenly black, darkening, with large slime green spots, and a wide body of black water. It reeked of swamp decay, stinking of swamp gases mixed with human excrement, even at this high altitude, and somewhere in the distance to his left, far off, a light, a flame erupted. The demon leveled off, and Militus prepared for his final move. He knew they were nearing the walls of Dis. He saw the huge, rusty metallic form appear.

Once over the wall, Militus could feel the heat wafting up from below. He had listened to the stories of Aristotle many, many times over the centuries, and he remembered the gruesome description of this area and its inhabitants being slowly burned alive. There was no way to describe the stench of the burning flesh rising out of the glowing tombs and caskets which lay below. The red, glowing patches on the ground indicated where the tormented were cooked alive. It was horrific to behold, even for the seasoned battle veteran.

In the distance, Militus saw the next circle approaching fast. The demon began to descend again, and Militus, defying the pain of moving his body with the broken leg, not to mention the painful claw-fingers of the demon flyer, flexed his torso upward, enough to get his hand into his belt pack. The demon looked down, and squeezed his claws tighter, pulling each of Militus' shoulders apart so hard that Militus thought he would be ripped apart, so strong was the beast. Militus grimaced and yelled as he felt his collarbone break. The demon cursed, and Militus made his daring move. With a painful flick of his wrist, he turned the knife he had grabbed from his belt into the bicep of the flyer, turning it as much as possible to maximize the damage and disable the beast. Screeching in pain, the demon squeezed the broken collarbone of Militus, but released his grip on the other shoulder. It slashed into the side of Militus' face, deeply lacerating him, and causing blood to flow heavily. Using the pain that was filling him, Militus slashed the knife again, but with a greater arc behind the blow. This time the demon howled with rage as its blood poured onto Militus' face, temporarily blinding him. The struggle in the air did not miss the attention of those below. The two were struggling, each trying to do as much damage as possible to the other; the demon was unable to do much except take each blow from Militus; its left arm was hanging, disabled because of the sinews cut by the veteran. It descended quickly, preparing to drop Militus and smash his body on the ground, disabling him until it could regenerate and finish the flight to the Eighth Circle. Militus, deciding that he would not like to drop, grabbed onto the hanging forearm of the beast, and flailed around until it had to land. The landing turned out to be its fatal mistake.

Both flyer and prisoner impacted on the ground. Bones smashed and broken, Militus was unable to move, and gasped as the wind had been knocked out of him once again. The demon, enraged beyond comprehension, was heavily damaged, but able to get up and round upon Militus' disabled, gasping body. Militus readied himself, waiting to be ripped apart and stared defiantly at the beast as it limped toward him. It began to ravage Militus, clawing his abdomen, ripping at his belly until it was opened and then shredding it into bloody pulp; the seasoned warrior gasped out screams and blood, choking and coughing in pain. The creature reveled in this power over his crippled prey, laughing in madness at the overpowering of the prisoner. It stood up tall, screeching in joy, ready for another round of bloodying, taunting Militus in his powerlessness.

"Foolish human. I will open up your – arghhhh!" The demon screeched, and many sickening thuds later, on the ground, flailing as it lay full of arrows. Militus could only turn his head now and watch. Over him, another creature was aiming its bow directly at his face. It was a centaur, but not Chiron. It pointed the arrow at the chest of Militus, and let it loose. Militus was blinded by the unbearable pain, unable to scream or breath. The next few moments were a fog for him, and he wished he could pass out from the pain, as he had from his last battle, when he was alive. Then a gruff voice sounded over all – he knew it was a centaur, because he had seen them, but it did not sound like Chiron's.

"Hold your arrows! Hold your arrows!" roared the voice. Moments later another centaur stood over Militus, and leaning over, pulled the arrow out of his chest. The centaur turned away, and began to yell at another. "We must inform Master Chiron. As for the filthy demon, keep filling its hide; do not let it escape. We will drag it to Master Chiron and the half-bull. Carry this one, who fights with demons."

"He is only a fugitive?" replied the other voice.

"Take him and do not question my authority or you will swim with Nessus!" roared the voice. Militus was quickly picked up, roughly, and thrown over the back of one of the centaurs, face down. This was a more proper way to transport a human and would not be considered a domestication of the centaur. The pain rolled through Militus in waves, and after a long, bumpy gallop, Militus noticed they were entering a grove of gnarled-looking trees as his head bumped up and down. He was still unable to move when they stopped, but he had regained his breath. Militus saw the demon writhing as it was dragged up behind them.

"Master Chiron – " said the centaur that was holding Militus. "This human was found on the bank. The demon and he were fighting in the air and fell to the bank. It had overtaken him before we arrived, but it was badly wounded by the human."

"I would see the human." said a familiar voice. A hand lifted Militus' head from the side of the centaur. It was Chiron.

"Militus!" exclaimed the Master centaur. "Gently take him off and place him onto the ground! He is to be treated with respect, a friend to our kind was he in life."

The centaur warriors lifted Militus, who expected their gentlest to still be quite rough, and was surprised at just how easily and painlessly he was placed on the ground. To his delight, Mortuus stood over him, smiling.

"Welcome Militus – it is good to see you again, though I am sorry to see you in the state you are in. The beast did quite a bit of damage," said Mortuus as Darius walked up alongside of him.

"You'd better pick weaker opponents to fight my friend," said the smiling Darius.

"Master Chiron," another voice, a centaur, that Militus did not know. "We thought him for a fugitive, and Theos sank an arrow into his chest before Master Pholus –"

"Leave me, now.' replied the unmistakable voice of Chiron. "You will spread the word to all your fellows. Do not attack any humans, even if you think them to be fugitives! Have Tacitus bring me the summoning horn."

"Yes, Master Chiron. I will tell all, especially Theos." And with that, Militus could hear the sound of the centaur galloping away. Mortuus and Darius were busy, ripping off pieces of their tattered robes and wiping the blood off of Militus.

Militus smiled weakly, for just a moment. Mortuus stepped away, and as Militus turned his head to the side, he beheld the ghastly sight of a pulverized human, barely breathing, crimson red in a bloody, pulpy mass. The head and side of the face were bleeding; it was covered in gore and what looked like brain matter coming out of some places. He turned away, the nightmare reminding him of some of the worst battles in his lifetime.

"Drink this Militus." Chiron poured a small vial of fluid into his mouth. It was bitter, and very bad tasting, but somehow Militus found it desirable. "This is one of the concoctions from Limbo, a fairly strong regenerative." Militus choked as he swallowed it down.

"Who is this lying next to me?" asked Militus.

"It is the teacher." replied Chiron.

"Oh no." said Militus, in surprise and anguish.

"Yes," said Chiron's voice, "That is Aristotle. We retrieved him, but he will need much time to regenerate. Now rest, Militus, and let your own regeneration occur." Militus was silent, and his friends sat near him as he closed his eyes and rested.

Chapter 63

The Fall of Limbo

In the time after the disappearance of Militus and the re-emergence of Socius and Barak from the cottage of the Chronicler, Limbo underwent a massive shift in theme. The great buildings were demolished. The Great Library, the Hall of Science, and the Amphitheatre were all destroyed in moments, as the Fallen made their appearance at the front of each building, uttered their incantations, and disappeared up into the misty ceiling as each structure fell into ruin. No warning was given to the occupants of the buildings or inhabitants of Limbo, and many people were trapped beneath the rubble and debris.

The Keep alone was spared, as was the Whirlpool Building. The individual cottages of the citizens of Limbo were searched and razed to the ground without exception. The warriors were attacked by hordes of demons, and their weaponry removed. Those who fought or spoke back were tied and tortured in plain sight of all outside the Keep as examples for the rest of the people. Many warriors fled toward the more deeply wooded sections of Limbo, hiding within the dense forests. Warriors who had any weapons hid them well. The other members of the citizenry were interrogated and ravaged by the demons randomly, ripped apart with the meat hooks and seized weaponry. In more extreme examples, the victims were taken to outer Hell and discarded.

The beginning of Limbo's fall saw the demons appearance within the populace. People who had known each other for centuries suddenly realized they had been infiltrated by the brutish, sadistic beasts. Terror filled them as friends and neighbors transformed into demons right before their eyes.

The paths around the Pool house were heavily guarded. None could pass unless accompanied by an Elder. Even then, the person might be interrogated and mutilated due to the normally violent nature of the demons. There was little comfort or reprieve for Limbo's people.

Clavius' laboratory was almost found after the demons had destroyed his cottage. They found the passage underneath and followed it to the end. Not seeing any visible exit other than the way they entered, they assumed it was not finished being dug. Clavius' neighbors were interrogated and tortured into giving away his identity. Clavius himself, aware that he was discovered, hid well, staying clear of demons and blending in to the crowds to avoid capture. The soldiers loyal to the disappeared Militus stayed nearby Clavius, flowing with the crowd whenever demons were sighted.

The mood of Limbo, once happier, with the smell of the grasses, woods and the general freedom of the people to move about and pursue their interests, became polluted with suspicion, brutality and fear as the Elders, reminding the populace that they had been warned for centuries about breaking the rules imposed upon them by the Fallen, walked about freely. They lorded their status, pointing out those who they did not like, for whatever reason, and that person was hauled off for torturing by the demons. They blamed Aristotle, and Socius and all others who had publicly discarded their 'wisdom' as the cause for the walking terror of the demon hordes.

The gates of Limbo were sealed shut, and according to the Elders, for good.

Chapter 64

Limbo for Beginners

I am convinced now, beyond a doubt that my life is a series of tests. I survived the mirror test of Hell, after waiting in a state of anxiety for what seemed too many days, though days and nights do not exist in Hell. The gray overcast remains very much static, and only the wind changed direction from time to time while I stood in the line.

I went before the mirror, in the same room with the centaur and Minos, both of whom are huge. The mirror sent me to Limbo, which left me in a state of relieved joy unlike any I had ever experienced in my lifetime. I ended up in a wooded area, a place between some small villages called Terni and Porto, respectively. The villages are located clockwise in Limbo, and the locals explained to me that the placement would be roughly one-hundred and eighty degrees from the path entrance into Limbo. The start of the path was where I had passed the door while in line, so I had apparently been sent very far away from the mirror. This was a good thing.

The trip was interesting, because I seemed to just be there, no sudden rush or stomach turning flight or bizarre science fiction spinning portal; time and space just bent around, and the walls of the hall became forest. There was a slight feeling that I had lost some time, like when you accidentally fall asleep; but I shrugged it off, since I had all the time I would ever need, and more. Minos was supposed to wrap his tail around me and toss me into some nasty pit of Hell, at least according to the story. But Minos did not have a tail; and I do not recall reading about centaurs being located so far up in Hell. Not to be too literal, I didn't expect this place to exist, but since it does, and I am sentenced to it, I would expect a bit of accuracy. Nevertheless, I felt I was the luckiest new dead guy in the universe after the mirror trick.

Things were going very well. In the forest, a large man and his smaller companion approached me, and I considered that to be a lucky break as well. At first I was scared, not knowing what was coming at me, and I tried to hide behind a tree, worried that some monstrous Hell-hounds were going to chase and eat me for eternity. They were strangely dressed, as are most of the people here, but they showed me how to get to the path and which way to go to find proper clothing. The death shroud cloth I came into Hell with was just too weird, even for a not-picky dresser like me. Polo shirts and jeans were my uniform of choice.

I reached the village of Porto some time later, enjoying the scents and smells of the wooded forest. Outer Hell had savaged my nostrils with its violence, and inhaling felt great. I wasn't hungry or thirsty, but being somewhat shy, some concern rose up as I arrived in the miniature village which turned out to not be a problem as I was quickly surrounded by the locals. They pressed me, asking questions suspicious of my identity. In fact, they were alerted to the presence of fugitives just before I arrived. The fugitives had been reported to have entered Limbo illegally and were wanted by the leaders of Limbo, some older folks known as the Elders Council. I happened into Limbo when all the interesting business of fugitives began.

Once the local villagers decided that I was absolutely not a fugitive, and my newer untarnished cloth assisted them in their decision, I was surrounded by men with makeshift tape measures, not manufactured types, but pretty good handmade versions that were actually more fancy looking. I was asked what styles of clothing I preferred, and said the same as I told the large man and his companion in the woods. Jeans.

Of course, the tailors had no idea what I was talking about. I was the first newcomer they had seen in many hundreds of years, which told me I was far luckier than I knew. But that meant they had never seen a pair of jeans in their lives, and that they had some method of telling time. In regards to my pants, I was able to pick out a material, and diagram a rough draft of a plain pair of jeans. They created several pairs, and I took one and put them on. The fit was good, and the material was very soft, weightless like spider web, but very strong for its lightness. They created a shirt and I happily removed most of the cloth I had come to Hell in. My new shirt was also light.

Finally, I finished talking and telling stories with these men; they were very generous, and the tailor who made the clothing I wore beamed as if he was the proud winner of the 'dress me' contest, smiling and lording his skills playfully at his tailor friends. I was pointed in the direction of Terni as the men thanked me for the visit. They wanted to share some wine to celebrate my coming into Limbo. As opposed to having been sentenced to anywhere in outer Hell, being sent to Limbo is a very big deal. I declined though because I was excited to see more of Limbo. The people had a great amount of time on their hands and they seemed to use their time very well. There was a library and an amphitheatre, and a building known as the Hall of Science which they recommended I see. They boasted of its giant height with its incredible four stories, the tallest building outside of the Keep, which was a castle that the Elders Council held meetings in. Honestly, I was happy just to have trees. I imagined Dante had either lied or exaggerated, or there had been a great deal of tree planting and construction in the last 700 years. The walls alone were quite an accomplishment, and I was glad to not have to breathe the air or see the outside of Limbo. As I left, the main tailor, the leader of the group, informed me that I might pass near a building that was situated on a large lake. He identified it as the Whirlpool building, and told me only to steer clear of it. 'Hug the inner wall' he said.

I passed through Terni later, and the people, like those who had surrounded me in Porto, looked at me, but did not attempt to interact. I expect my clothing had a great deal to do with this, but I was feeling good, and did not try to stop and chat. The woods were always my comfort, even in my life, and I continued on, sighing every so often at the good fortune to have landed in Limbo. The Whirlpool building came up some time after Terni, and I veered to the left path nearest the inner wall. I stepped up my pace, and passed through quickly. As I watched the building, I saw in the distance something big fly up and out from the other side, nearer the outer wall that bordered the river Acheron. It was human shaped, and fast, and disappeared over the trees that were in front of me. The flapping was hard, like meat being hit with a wide hammer. It was a signature wing beat that I would recognize many more times. In fact, another of the creatures flew over and past me not so long after in the same general direction. I continued walking, hoping I would not see the beasts again while alone. I was quite shaken, and had not realized it.

Much, much later, the forest thinned out, to my dismay. It reminded me of my trek with my family. We took a road trip once and were enjoying the rocky wilderness of Colorado for some time in our drive. Later, the trees thinned, then disappeared and we were in the northern hills and desert, with only minor brush filling for trees. This was how I felt as I approached the mines. The locals of Porto had told me as much, but I was daydreaming as I walked through the forest, and enjoying the long, peaceful surrounding of wilderness. The landscape became sparsely treed, then flat and rocky.

It was empty, except for the tall walls on either side of me. In the distance, large piles of rocks blocked my view. As I got nearer to the piles, another of the flying creatures passed over, flying directly over the rock piles. It looked as though it dropped down behind the heap. I stood still, feeling some amount of dread. I got a better view of the creature, and I did not like what I saw; it was an odd, purplish color, its face like some gnarled tree knot, twisted in anger. The beast was very well muscled, appearing very powerful in build. I looked at it emotionlessly, but inside, I was actually trembling. I stood still for a long time, trying to gather any semblance of courage I might need. Finally I began my walking, deciding I would just have to work around an encounter with it as best I could, Surely the people here had to deal with the beasts once in a while. And I was very curious at the same time, so I wanted to have a closer look.

A path was made through the piles, easy to see, and I followed it. It was a strange path, but I followed as it opened into a wide pit, with concentric circles that wrapped around and down to a central area with an entrance to a mine. Across from me, a bunch of people were sitting or laying on the ground, and I noticed the two guys, one very big and his friend who had directed me to Porto. Interestingly, there was the centaur again, but he appeared to be bleeding, and in fact, all of the people here looked a little beaten, even from as far away as I was.

Honestly, I turned around and walked back behind the rocks; I was too new here to be scrapping already, especially since I did not know who the good guys were. And just what was this centaur doing here? *Dante must have had his head in his goddamned ass*, I thought angrily. I was scared, and when scared, I complain.

I had no idea what to do, so I stayed put until sometime later, when a small band of men came around the corner of the rock pile. They were armed with bows and arrows, spears, and actual real long swords!

"Halloo stranger." said one of them. The others looked at me, waiting for my reply.

"Hi." I said this shyly, still stunned at the weaponry.

"You would be wise to remain here for the moment, stranger. There may be trouble coming. Did you witness the earlier attack?" I shook my head; I knew something had happened here.

"No, though I saw injured people, and the centaur around the pit."

"Yes. Even Master Chiron was not spared this round."

"Chiron?" I said. The centaur was Chiron? "Chiron? Really?"

"Yes. Master Chiron hails from the Seventh Circle, on business of his own." replied the man. "He and the others were on their way out of Limbo when the demon attacked." And now I was quite enthralled.

"That purplish flying thing was a *demon*?" I said.

"Yes. Frightening, are they not?" I was once again stunned. Weren't demons red with horns? Jesus this is a weird place.

"Very," I answered. I was relieved he seemed as fearful as I did. "What happened to it? I didn't see it in the pit, only those wounded."

"It has been destroyed." said the man.

"Destroyed? How do you destroy a demon, if I may ask? I thought they would be eternal here ...being it's Hell and all."

"Suffocation, or if you impale them rapidly enough. They are very very strong, so no human can best them. Only recently have we seen one perish at the hands of Mortuus. There is one other way-" He was cut off by another.

"Appis. Use your discretion."

"Yes. Of course." he said. "I will not burden you with too much information in case you are questioned. Where do you normally dwell, stranger?" He had changed the subject.

"I am a new arrival and just finding my way around. I was on my way to the Library."

"Ahh, then welcome to Limbo stranger. What is your name?"

"I am John Moore. Is there some other way around this pit I am unaware of Appis?"

"No, John Moore, there is only the way through the pit. In a few minutes you may go. Have you washed in the waters yet?"

"I passed but I did not wash. Why do you ask?"

"The waters are quite healing to drink, and will wash the stench of outer Hell if you bathe. "

"Interesting. I will see to it when I pass again. I hope I do not offend."

"You do not, I only wished to share the knowledge of the waters. You will pass another before you reach the Hall of Science. It is advisable that you bathe on the part of the water that opens to the path first. The rapids of the far end are too perilous, and may cause you injury."

"Thank you for that. I will bathe then before I reach the Library."

"You are welcome." I noticed the others of Appis' party were looking up into the air, like they expected more of the demons to fly in.

"Appis, why is it the demons are coming? Has something happened?"

"It is a long story," he replied, "and should not concern you. The beasts will not find what they seek, and all will return to normal soon."

"What do they seek?" But Appis only smiled and looked up into the air like his friends. I looked up, then parted from the men. I crossed the pit around its edge to the far side, where a similar path exited and continued my walk.

This was a strange land of mysteries. Luckily, I had plenty of time on my hands.

Chapter 65

Emergence

"Socius – where would you like to be returned to?" asked Avius. The Chronicler was browsing in one of his large spell books, perusing the incantations he could use to return Barak and Socius back to Hell.

"I took it for granted we would return to your cottage Master Avius?" Socius had a puzzled look on his face. Avius, not looking up from his opened tome, paused for a moment. Barak looked at Avius curious. The three had walked into the mirror within the cottage of Avius and come to a large room with many books; it was the library of the Chronicler, a very rare visit by an outsider, as Barak had told Socius on many occasions. Barak had been to the vast book collection of the Chronicler before, but his visit was very short, and the chronicler had blindfolded him. He had waited many centuries for this visit, and he did not wish to leave. The tomes, giant bound volumes in aged fabric, were full of information about Hell, angel magic, and so many other topics that Barak could spend years savoring the data within. The only problem was the language. Each tome of the angel magic and lore was written in the language of the Angelics, which no one, except the Chronicler himself understood. Socius was indifferent to the texts and their value, despite the multiple repeated attempts by Barak to explain it to him. Finally, in frustration, Barak gave up his efforts. The Chronicler taught him some spells, simple angel magic that would be of more use when he returned to Limbo.

Upon their entry, Socius had asked where the three were. Avius told him.

"You are in the library. More precisely, a deep sub-basement of the Great Library." Socius was dumbfounded.

"How can this be? We were fully on the far side of Limbo."

"The portal can be set to transport us to many places Socius."

"I see no doorways to the upper floors. How do you get to the exit?"

"There are no passages out of here except for the mirror itself, Socius. It is unfortunate for Barak since he has to get me many books from the Great Library. It would be far quicker to install a stairway. But it would also provide access to my own library, which I cannot allow."

"How did you build this room? How deep under the library are we?"

"It is almost as deep as the library is high, Socius. I did not trust my skills at using the mining spells to create this large room, so I started deep. Happily, the upper library was not harmed during my dig."

"Very impressive. A very good hiding place right under the noses of the Elders. No wonder no one can find you." Socius was in awe. They had stayed in this underground for a lengthy period though and he was about ready to leave. "Can we return to the field by your cottage?"

"Limbo has undergone some unfortunate changes since we left, my friends. I did not wish to tell you, but it was probably caused by my 'interaction' with the demons that were attacking you. The spell I cast to remove them was a bit noticeable, apparently."

"Remove them? But they were shrieking very loudly, as if they were in pain. I thought you had destroyed them. Where did you send them?" asked Barak.

"Back to their creators, of course." Socius stood agape, then Barak chimed in.

"Their creators? The Fallen?"

"Yes. They are not appreciated by their Fallen masters either, especially in their private area. They will cause much havoc, and eventually be removed or destroyed."

"Could you not just destroy them?" asked Socius.

"Yes. However, I prefer not to. My solution is far better. Wish I could have been there to enjoy it." Avius smiled as Socius and Barak stood in shock, then laughed heartily.

"You have an unusual sense of humor, Avius." chuckled Socius.

"Indeed." added Barak.

"Where do the Fallen reside?" asked Socius.

"Winged creatures live in aeries, of course," stated Avius, matter-of-factly. Socius wore a look of puzzlement.

"Where?" asked Socius. "I am very curious."

"That will be revealed to you soon enough, youngling. Now, returning to my question – where would you like to be returned to?"

"I have my reasons, Barak. Socius will need your assistance when you leave here. And for where you are going, you will need his protection. I'll ask you two again. Where would you like to return to? Limbo is not the same place you left, and the demons may be expecting you to return in close proximity to my cottage." Socius pondered this for a few moments.

" Do you mean outer Hell? I am not certain where we should go, Avius. I have barely been outside of Limbo myself, and I really did not like the experience. Do you have some recommendation? I will tell you, I am a bit fearful of the outside, yet I have always wanted to go to see it." Socius reminisced. "I had expected to go with Aristotle, but…then he never returned."

"Very well. I will send you to Phlegyas; he can guide you to the centaurs where you will be safe. You will have to protect Barak, Socius. He is a clever student, but as a warrior, I think he comes up a bit short. Phlegyas liked Aristotle, so be certain to mention his name when you two meet. He will surely help on your journey. You do remember Phlegyas, from Aristotle's stories?"

"Yes of course. The oarsman of Styx, the swamp surrounding Dis." answered Socius. Barak nodded. He had read many of Aristotle's accounts of his travels, and he was familiar with the various workers of outer Hell.

"Good. Now," Avius placed his hands together, interlocking his fingers, "Prepare for the portal opening. Socius, you have packed the regeneration potions for Mortuus?" Socius nodded and held his pack up. "Good. I will see you again, Barak. You have been a faithful student, keeping my secret for many centuries. Both of you will need to find Mortuus; remember, he is in need of one of the large vials. These remedies are only for the worst needs of regeneration. When Mortuus begins the change, stay with him. It is very painful." Avius was stern on this point, his face revealing the seriousness. He bent over his tome, reading again, then, looked at the pair.

"Do not move until I signal you. Once you arrive at the edge of the swamp, look for the signal tower and do not enter the swamp. Prepare yourselves." He read aloud. "*Basqi ites mufeza'viaeta...como unlni rasz!*" The mirror on the far wall began to glow, a luminescent bluish light pouring out for a moment, then smoothing out into a lighter blue, an aqua glass. "Walk through together. Good luck my friends!" he shouted.

Socius and Barak turned and stepped into the widened mirror as the odor of fetid, stinking swamp filled their nostrils.

Chapter 66

The Encounter

Phlegyas was a large, sinewy tangle of angry muscle, not an ounce of body fat to smooth the knotted strings. Socius, still reeling from the revelations of the Chronicler, studied the oarsman, comparing this real Phlegyas to his own previously imagined version. This Phlegyas was more intimidating, and his booming voice alone had frightened Barak when they first met. Phlegyas had been less than friendly, but warmed considerably when Socius identified himself. Barak was shaken up and shied away from the brusque oarsman; outer Hell was always only a theory; the true experience was very much overwhelming for the student of Avius. He imagined it must have been quite a rude awakening for Mortuus.

Phlegyas pushed the skiff along slowly, wanting to maximize his time with the friendly company; they were going to the rear entrance of Dis that earlier Mortuus, Chiron and Darius had been transported to. Of late, the transport's passengers were all demons and imps, and their ill tempers had caused them to rake Phlegyas on more than one occasion.

The imps were particularly troublesome, not willing to sit still, and almost discovered Phlegyas' private stash. One imp had been pulled overboard by a small contingent of angry swamp-dwelling humans, making its demon master so angry, it ripped at Phlegyas' back and chest several times.

"Phlegyas – I have noticed your wounds. Have you been attacked recently?" asked Barak, trying to overcome his fear. Phlegyas had caught Barak's aversion to him, and decided to taunt him in jest.

"Yes. What of it, peon!" yelled the oarsman. Phlegyas stared at Barak in mock anger for a minute, as Barak slowly backed up as far as possible from him within the skiff before finally bursting out into hearty laughter. "Do not fear me boy, truly, I am on your side. The demons have been at me for some time, and I am transporting many demons since the awakening of Mortuus. Far removed from their Fallen lords, their temperament is more horrid than Hell itself. I cannot get them across this swamp fast enough."

Barak, relieved, looked at Socius who was smiling at Phlegyas' joke.

"I believe we have enough water to spare some for our humorous guide, Socius. What do you say?" asked Barak.

"Absolutely. I have heard you assisted Mortuus as well, Phlegyas? We are in your debt. Limbo is astir now; Mortuus has been long waited for by many, though I have only found this out recently." Barak passed two large vials to Socius, who extended them to Phlegyas. Phlegyas smiled as he took the waters.

"Many thanks, friends. What of Limbo, Socius? The Fallen are angered at Mortuus escape? Chiron said the demons had infiltrated the place, and that some demons have been there all along."

"Limbo is filthy with the beasts, Phlegyas. They replaced an Elder, and many of my own friends, students of the Chronicler. Who knows where else the beasts are lurking. Our secret society, unknown even to me until recently, seems to have also been infiltrated." Phlegyas pondered this.

"If they have gained so many places in Limbo, then they must have taken those they replaced to lower Hell. It is the most difficult to escape; it is patrolled by dark devils, more dangerous and twisted than the demons and imps, who will not go there unless directed by Fallen."

"How do you come by this information Phlegyas?" asked Barak.

"I am here many, many centuries my friends. Until I met Aristotle, I had no one to speak to except fugitives and demons. As for the fugitives I am required to alert the Fallen masters; but surprisingly, I rarely ever do. As for the demons, they talk amongst themselves or not at all. The flyers carry their captives to the lower pits and according to what I have heard, they throw their prisoners on top of the unsuspecting devils as their own sort of entertainment."

"Do you know anything of the pits, Phlegyas?" inquired Socius.

"I have heard stories from the fugitives. One told me there are many pits, some of fire, boiling pitch, rivers of stinking shit, flesh eating monsters, though differing from the imps, and all serviced by the dark devils. This particular escapee hailed from a pit where he wallowed in human excrement and he said that pit was the easiest to escape. The beasts rarely go near it because of the smell, and he was ripe with it. When he escaped, the devils in the next pit spotted him. He had to stand under a waterfall of hot red water to hide; like the demons, each had a lengthened meat hook. Although burned badly, he was grateful for the cleaning, though he stilled stunk. I would have thrown him into the Styx if I had not been longing for some human company. It's just as well I let him go. He was eventually caught - I saw them flying over and I knew from the stench it was he," Barak shuddered.

"As if the normal smell of outer Hell was not enough. The red waterfall?" asked Barak. "I recall it from Aristotle's travel logs. It falls from the blood rill. But how did the fugitive get past the flying monster?"

"The monster is Geryon." said Phlegyas. "The guardian of the Eighth Circle – it patrols the outer rim. It is some sort of bastardized creature, and is quite vicious. The tail is that of a scorpion, and if it stings you, the poison lasts for some time. The poison inhibits regeneration, and burns as it courses through your body. The demons are terrified of the beast, and apparently it is not fond of them either." Phlegyas paused. "I received a sting from this beast. It took almost a century for the burning to completely cease."

"Why did you get stung by the monster way? The Eighth Circle is far from here." asked Socius.

"I attempted to escape." replied Phlegyas. Socius and Barak looked at the oarsman in shock. "The beast caught me climbing down the wall near the rill. It stung me and threw me out onto the burning plain. I lay on the burning sand until I could crawl back to the rill, then worked my way back here."

"*You* attempted escape?" asked the astonished Barak. "But you are a worker. Why woul-"

"I am a prisoner, just as you," said the oarsman. "Only now it will become obvious to you that you are as much a prisoner as any other in this place. Now that your pleasant stay in Limbo has been compromised, you will see the extent of your punishment. Did you not ever wonder, in all your centuries, that there might be something more?"

"But what did you hope for, Phlegyas?" asked Barak. "You might have become one of the tortured…"

"Indeed. But Hell was young, and the torments were not all in place yet. The Fallen had not finished building their 'kingdom'. I had hoped for an exit below. I had already tried to leave by the entrance in the Vestibule to no avail. Geryon was a surprise."

"Darius and his two fellow fugitives tried that escape too. We understand," said Socius.

The skiff neared the greenish red rusty metal walls of Dis. Socius and Barak had read of Aristotle's description of the entombed, eternally roasted and the moans came from this circle. They heard the moaning and smelled the scent of burning flesh from across the swamp; now the pained sounds were louder, and the odor more offensive.

"My friends" said Phlegyas. "We have reached the back entrance to Dis. Prepare for the gruesome experience of the burning city of tombs. It is quite a horrific experience from what you are used to, and I am afraid you may swoon, overwhelmed. Aristotle had a great deal of trouble his first time through, and I expect you will also." Socius and Barak saw only weathered, rusty metal and rivets as they docked against the wall; it appeared to be the same as any other panels. As Phlegyas spoke the combination spell, an outline formed in the metal, shaping into a small doorway.

"Pass through the doorway together. Once through, you must head as straight away from the wall as the tomb configuration will allow. There is no returning through this way – only the front gate, located clear on the other side of the circle, is usable for that. Pull your packs tight and wield your weapons. Whatever may be on the other side, you will have no choice but to fight it. You have no time to get used to the heat from the tombs or the stench of burning flesh that fills the air in Dis. Farewell, my friends. Until we meet again. Go, now!"

The two pushed through the doorway, falling to the ground on the other side. The heat came in waves, but the odor turned out to be far more brutal. They had tried to emotionally prepare for the sounds of suffering and pain, but the actual sight was frightening beyond their expectation. Barak froze up, starting to go into a paralyzed shock, and Socius, not faring well himself, focused on getting his friend through the nightmarish landscape; it was his willpower that pushed them through the tombs unceasingly. Once they faltered, slipping against a glowing casket, and burned themselves badly. The pain seemed to pull Barak from his stunned state, and the two walked faster, not stopping until they had reached the rocky slope that led down into the circle of the centaurs.

The coppery smell of the boiling river was the newest odor to assault their noses as they walked down the slope; that, mixed with the smell of the burning flesh became a disturbing new stench. It was repulsive, and the newcomers to outer Hell now fully understood the bravery which Aristotle had to have in order to leave Limbo.

A large centaur patrol saw the pair walking down the slope. A company of twenty-five centaurs trotted uphill to intercept the pair, as one centaur raced toward the area where Chiron and Pholus stayed with the recently rescued humans. Barak was surprised by the speed of the centaurs. Fortunately for Socius and Barak, Chiron had ordered his centaurs not to harm any humans. The commander of the company watched as Socius bowed to him, keeping his head down until the centaur returned the gesture. This caused a curiosity among the herd, and they began to question Socius.

"Who are you and why are you here?" asked the commander.

"I am Socius, and this is Barak," said Socius. 'We are come to meet with Master Chiron. We have come from the circle of Limbo. We are friends."

"How do you know of our customs, young human?" asked the centaur.

"I learned your custom from my mentor," answered Socius. Aristotle had taught him to bow, letting the centaurs know he meant only respect. The leader signaled to the other centaurs, and they stood in formation.

"We shall take you to Master Chiron, humans. Follow us."

And off they went to meet Chiron.

Chapter 67

Changing Priorities

Only Pholus, the human Panos, and four centaurs remained in the hiding place in the Wood, standing over the regenerating fleshy pulp of the unknown human, the one who had not been given the healing waters. Chiron, Darius, the mostly regenerated Aristotle, Militus and Mortuus went off to the rill. Chiron took them to explore the Seventh Circle, crossing the burning-sand of the fiery plain, all the way to the cliff edge where the rill dropped its boiling liquid down to the Eighth Circle. Pholus, like most of the centaurs, would not venture too near to the fire of the plain. Panos, having suffered on the plain for a length of time before escaping to the Wood, chose to stay with Pholus and the herd. Asterion had befriended a small company of centaurs, and he decided to walk along with them, talking as they patrolled the Wooded side of the Seventh Circle.

Pholus went out to meet the newest strangers from Limbo before allowing them to see the hiding space within the trees. The strangers smiled as they were gently lowered to the ground by the centaur that had carried them across Phlegethon's shallows.

"I am Pholus, second to Master Chiron. Identify yourselves, and tell us why you come this way." Pholus was very stern and commanded respect with his direct approach and generally strong poise. He was as large as Chiron, though slightly rougher in appearance facially. He appeared somewhat more sensitive and intelligent than the centaurs who had met the pair on the slope.

"I am Socius, and this is Barak. We are friends of Aristotle, acquaintances to Master Chiron," said Socius, quite formally. "We seek Master Chiron." Socius smiled as he said this, knowing he was dealing with another of Aristotle's contacts in this circle. Pholus was well known from the travel logs.

"I have heard of you, Socius, through my encounters with Aristotle. Chiron has recently mentioned your name, Barak, in his travel to Limbo. You are both most welcome to our circle. We are hosting quite a few outsiders these days." The second centaur and the visitors from Limbo finished their introductions, gradually warming as they shared their individual stories. The conversation continued uniformly, until the mass of bloody, raw flesh on the ground behind

Pholus shuddered, and in an instant the mixed party of Halflings, Limbo's refugees and the fugitive Panos was thrown into tree branches, trunks, and each other, smashed so hard that some of their bones were sticking out through their skin.

A quiet explosion had occurred in their midst, and they were all in shock from the noiseless concussion. Barak was sent high into a tree, caught in its branches as overhead a flock of harpies, previously unseen, but apparently there the whole time, took to flight, screeching in fear and panic. A lone centaur trotted into the place where Panos, who had been standing over the mutilated human, stood seconds before. The unknown, looking painfully up at the centaur, began to moan in a deathly fear. The human could still barely speak or move since the rescue from the forbidden area cave. The centaur looked at the raw flesh, and pulling out a large meat hook, slung it into the bloody mass, then turned and walked away, dragging the faintly crying form out toward the river. The stunned centaurs, battered and bleeding, could only watch in pain, groaning as they tried to regain their mobility. They were deafened by the trees which were now screeching from being struck by the party.

Socius, the least damaged of the entire group, dropped down from a tree, landing on his feet, though still dazed. A tree branch stuck through into his lower leg, and he swore as he slowly pulled it out. Getting up as quickly as he could, he followed the rogue centaur and the mystery human being towed behind the centaur.

"Centaur!" yelled Socius. The centaur did not turn or flinch in response. Socius looked harder at the centaur; it seemed to be unraveling before his eyes. "Centaur!!" Socius yelled louder then got an idea. "Filthy half-breed! I challenge you! Walk away then – run!" As Socius said this, Pholus limped up behind him, battered and bloody.

"Centaur!! Stop now! I command you!" Pholus yelled. The centaur did not flinch, or make any acknowledgement of Pholus as it kept dragging its bloody cargo, leaving a trail on the ground. It was nearing the river, and soon would be dragging the body across. A company of centaurs approaching in the distance were staring, not aware of what had just happened. Pholus motioned them to come hastily The centaur that was dragging the human away stopped. It considered the approaching herd, then turned in the direction of Pholus and Socius.

"Demon. I see you. You are not worthy to wear that form." said Socius, turning to Pholus. "That is no centaur, Pholus."

"Though my eyes deceived me, my nose did not." The demon centaur raised its hands, waving them as it reverted into its true form. It spread its wings in a sudden display, enlarging itself, trying to scare off the approaching centaurs.

"It is going to fly off!" yelled Socius as he boldly ran at the demon. The herd was galloping quickly toward the demon, readying their bows along the way. Pholus could barely walk.

"Socius, stand back. The herd will take care of the demon!" Socius stopped and the demon placed its hook back into the immobilized human form. It spread its wings wide and began to beat them rapidly. In an instant, its wings filled with arrows, some penetrating fully and others remaining stuck in the wing and the back of the demon. It shrieked and turned toward the galloping herd. An arrow appeared within its throat and no more sounds emitted from it. Choking and bloody, it fell to the ground, writhing in pain. Socius walked up to it and repeatedly stabbed it with his long knife until it stopped moving. Moments later it was a cloud of smoke, and dissipated rapidly, carried away by the heat of the river Phlegethon.

Pholus, in utter, joyous, disbelief, walked into the circle. A smallish centaur traveling with the herd was summoned by Pholus.

"Titan," asked Pholus of the youthful Halfling, "do you fear the flames of the plain?" Titan thought about the question for a moment, and replied hesitantly.

"I do, Master Pholus, why –"

"I need a brave youngling to seek out Master Chiron and his acquaintances; they are traveling on the rill, though they may be near to getting back. Will you perform the task? Titan did not hesitate in his reply.

"Yes, Master Pholus. But the Wood may be –" Pholus cut him off.

"I would not send you into danger, Titan. I want you to tell Tacitus to accompany you to the edge of the Wood, where the rill meets the flaming desert. They are to stay there until you return. Is that acceptable?" asked Pholus.

"Very much so, Master Pholus."

"Good. Make haste, courageous Titan. Tell Master Chiron this is an urgent matter." Titan did not wait to be told twice, he began a gallop toward the rill, where he knew to find Commander Tacitus and his company. Pholus turned toward the company of centaurs standing around Socius.

"Go, and assist our brothers in the Wood – they were hurt badly by the demon's spell." They left as Pholus looked at the mass of human that had been the cause of the magical attack. "You are apparently a very important prisoner of the Fallen, human. We will need to hide you much better. We have underestimated your importance." Pholus, examining the important prisoner, took hold of the meat hook, and carefully, gently, removed it. Socius walked over to the shredded mass.

"I have something to help regenerate this one more quickly if you like, Master Pholus. The Chronicler gave me some of his herbal medicines and instructions for their use. We can speed up his healing greatly, which I would recommend – he looks very, very bad; it is painful to look at his condition."

"Excellent Socius. Please do whatever you can; we need to find out why this one is of such value to the Fallen." Socius opened his pack and began treating the important prisoner of the Fallen. He had expected the healing and regeneration to take several hours. Within minutes of application, the wounded prisoner was able to speak, and another few minutes saw the previously mutilated man become whole right before their eyes. Pholus and Socius could only stare in disbelief as the wounds closed and bones restructured themselves before their eyes. It was a miraculous event to behold, and Pholus wished Chiron had been here to witness it. The Master Centaur was also a master medicine maker, and this would interest him to no end.

Chiron, Mortuus, Darius, Aristotle, and Militus returned at once; Aristotle, seeing Socius once again, was overcome, and their reunion was as a father and son event, each weeping joyously, as if Aristotle had returned from the dead, which he had. Shortly after, Asterion returned, having heard of the attack from centaurs they passed while on patrol. He was running, angry for leaving his friend behind, more relieved when he saw that Chiron was unharmed. The group was huddled around another human, whom Asterion could not see until he got closer. When he was near enough, he could see he did not recognize the human.

"It is good to see you again, my friend," said Chiron to Asterion. Asterion nodded happily, but the half-bull was staring around at the new faces of Socius and Barak, and particularly at the man in the middle of the gathering.

"Who are these new faces? Who is this one?" grunted the Minotaur. Pholus, Chiron, Militus and Socius looked at each other momentarily, then back at Asterion and the stranger. Barak and Panos, still injured, and sitting on the ground, studied the stranger curiously.

Chiron spoke, "First, Asterion, I would introduce you to Socius and Barak, who have arrived here just now from Limbo." Socius and Barak smiled at Asterion, but the half-bull stared at them grimly. He was quite fierce in appearance, whether that was his preferred countenance or not. Chiron continued, "I will start the questioning of our unknown guest now."

The mystery man, short, uni-browed, and very thin, like a half-starved wretch, sat in the midst of the assemblage, looking around fearfully, shy and insecure of this strange band of his rescuers. He was breathing nervously, and his eyes, which were darting from face to face, settled on Mortuus. He was drawn inexorably to this large stranger's strong yet gentle appearance without question because it was easier on the eyes and disposition than the intense stares of the centaurs or the half-bull. The Minotaur was staring a hole through him.

Chiron prodded, "Who are you human? What is your name?" The thin man looked down, unsure of his own ability to use his voice. He was not quite clear-headed or free from perhaps centuries of disorientation. Finally, with great effort, swinging his head around to meet all their eyes, he croaked out his reply.

"I am Dante...Dante Alighieri."

To be continued in

AngelFall
Book IV

Available July 2012

CPSIA information can be obtained at www.ICGtesting.com
Printed in the USA
LVOW06s1502140713

342805LV00021B/818/P